MW01172979

Punks4Palestine

An Anthology of Hopeful SciFi

for an Uncertain Future

A Charity Anthology Benefiting

Doctors Without Borders

Edited and with an introduction by

Jasen Bacon

Featuring Stories by

R.J. Breathnach   Emma Burnett

Eric Farrell   Abigail Guerrero

May Haddad   J.D. Harlock   Toshiya Kamei

Christopher R. Muscato   Marc Ruvolo

Moe Shalabi   R. L. Summerling

Cover Art by Logan O'Connor

Punks4Palestine

A HyphenPunk Anthology

Copyright © 2024 HyphenPunk

First Published in the United States by HyphenPunk

The authors of the individual stories retain the copyright of the works featured in this anthology.

This is a collection of works of fiction. Names, characters, places, and incidents either are the product of the authors' imaginations or are used fictitiously. Any resemblance to any actual persons, living or dead, as well as events or locales are entirely coincidental.

All rights reserved. No part of this may be reproduced, stored in a retrieval system, or transmitted by any means, electronic, recording, mechanical, photocopying, or otherwise without the prior written permission of the publisher and copyright owners.

ISBN (paperback): 979-8-9908835-1-2

ISBN (ebook): 979-8-9908835-0-5

This book is dedicated to all the selfless doctors,

Nurses, and other medial professionals

who knowingly put themselves in danger

in the face of horrors, both natural and manmade,

to aid humanity.

CONTENTS

Introduction

I was shocked and appalled by Israel's disproportionate response to the attacks of October 7th, 2023. It sent me into a spiral of depression that my meds couldn't handle. I felt hopeless. What could one poor punk in the hills of East Tennessee do in the face of such horror? Then it hit me. I help people make books, so why not make one of my own.

On October 24th, 2023 I posted on social media I was going to publish a charity anthology, this charity anthology you are now reading. Looking at the devastation that was going on, and Israel's targeted attacks on hospitals, it was clear to me that medical aid was in desperate need. Doctors Without Borders became the obvious choice for the charity.

I have been a long fan and supporter of Doctors Without Borders. Their work in over 70 countries has brought relief to many people who need it the most. They even set up and helped in the United States during the Covid-19 pandemic. That is more indicative of the utter thrash that is the American medical system than anything.

We must also remember that Palestine is not the only ongoing genocidal event in the world today. In addition to Gaza, Doctors Without Borders are already on the ground in The Democratic Republic of Congo, Sudan, Ethiopia, Yemen, Armenia, and more places where people are facing horrible disasters and atrocities. Even after these crises are mediated, more are sure to come.

1

PUNKS4PALESTINE

By purchasing this book you are doing a part to help
Doctors Without Borders keep up their mission. All
proceeds from this book are being donated to the
charity so that all who are suffering can find some hope.
That is why this anthology is a collection of hopeful scifi.
While we know that the world is full of horrors, we must
also look to the future with optimism.

-Jasen Bacon

Ride On, Shooting Star

By May Haddad

Carna's Cerva had just enough fuel to reach the Narra Harbor. But as she struggled to maneuver her scooter through the cosmic turbulence she realized that, for the first time in her career as a courier, she was running on empty. Securing her grappling hook against the nearest comet, she landed on its surface as gently as she could, then lay back and let gravity handle the rest. If she was lucky she could hitch a ride without refilling her tank.

Earlier, Carna' had gone missing and needed to be tracked down to the resto-cafe at the other end of the universe. Though she was never one for alcohol, Carna' could always drink her problems away here at the Leafs of Lebanon. Except, that is, on the night that would've been her thirtieth birthday back on Earth, where she just sat at the counter, contemplatively staring down at the crystal glass in her hands as old Fairuz songs played in the background.

Expecting the worst when her supervisor Achut arrived with the return order stamped by the Courier-Master General herself, Carna' was surprised to see him sit down quietly beside her instead and casually order tabbouleh and drinks. The man seemed to be minding his own business, and for the first time, Carna' noticed that his carved face had furrowed since she had first

3

met him, giving him more distinguished features that had aged him beyond his years.

"You've finally joined me for a meal," Carna' mused out loud, hoping to end the prolonged silence that seemed to dictate their conversations. However, her manager chose not to reply, enjoying his salad silently, seemingly unconcerned with having to clock back in on time.

"You know…" Achut finally remarked, sipping at a shot of arak after the tabbouleh was picked to the last shred of parsley. "Ever since you told me about this dish, I'd been meaning to try it when — if I ever made it back to Earth. But this might be my last chance… for a while…"

Carna' leaned in playfully. "Finally saved up enough for a vacation?"

"No," Achut dabbed his mouth with a napkin. "Not that I'm looking forward to leaving the UCS to become a shipping super." He then studied his watch, looking like he was fighting the urge to get up and go. "Moving on to more of the same isn't what I had in mind when I thought I'd finally get the chance to leave this job, but the husband and I are looking to adopt, and I can't afford to be doing this in my forties."

Carna' drunkenly rested her chin on her palm.

"Come on, being a courier's not that bad."

"You mean the low pay, long hours, and nonexistent benefits aren't that bad."

"Well, maybe a little."

4

"Like you, I signed up to be a courier because the final frontier was where I had to be, and money was an object. But, having done this for over a decade now, I wonder why I thought it would be any different than Earth."

"But, chasing me down's not so bad."

Achut opened his mouth to say something clever but seemed to reconsider before looking around the resto-café with a tinge of regret in his eyes and said, "Yeah." He sighed, "Maybe it's not.."

To think that Carna's fading nation could be found all the way across the known universe was as remarkable to her as her being here — here, instead of the monotony of life back in southern Lebanon after the last of the civil wars ended when she was a child. Though she found herself comforted by the familiarity of the establishment she was in, this served little to quell the profound wistfulness that had set in.

"I wish I could come here whenever I wanted."

"I'm sorry management felt the need to 'limit' your mobility after the last couple of 'detours.'"

"Come to think of it, this job was fine before that." Carna' buried her head in her hands and groaned. "You know — if you don't overthink the low pay, long hours, and nonexistent benefits. Being a courier meant there were places to be, people to meet, and all the adventure you could ever want out of life."

5

"Honestly, I've been meaning to ask for a while." Achut removed his spectacles and ran his hand over his face, rubbing his eyes. "But why haven't you left yet?"

Carna' was taken aback.

"What do you mean," she asked, confused.

Achut turned away from her with a tinge of embarrassment.

"You seem miserable," he replied after a moment of silence.

Carna' frowned, but she understood why he'd asked. "I'm not sure. I'm having trouble figuring it out myself. Something doesn't feel right about leaving this life. I mean, what else would I do? Where else would I go?"

Achut sighed again. "It's going to be a pain. But…" He paused, looking like he wasn't sure if he wanted to propose something. "Before I vacate the position, I can sign off on an all-expenses-paid vacation that'll let you head back home. Of course, you'll have to spend most of it delivering packages to some of the most unsavory places on the planet, but it'll all be worth it with the low pay, long hours, and nonexistent benefits."

Carna' laughed. "Sounds lovely." Then she closed her eyes and tried to imagine what life would be like for her back on the farm. "Maybe…"

Now lost in her own thoughts (and five shots of arak), Carna' was on the verge of falling asleep when Achut suddenly snapped his fingers, bringing her back to the Leafs of Lebanon.

"I just remembered..." Achut seemed to speak sheepishly now. "There's one last assignment on your schedule before I can send you back. But... if you'd like, I can reassign it to —"

"No."

As Carna' made her way to one of the military stations off the moons of Resheph, she was surprised to find that her destination was not an outpost but one of the compounds that housed the families of those in service. These required less stringent background checks and pat-downs, but the sight of soldiers was all the same unsettling.

Parking her Cerva in one of the stations designated for guests, she entered the compound anxiously only to be caught off guard by the immaculate presentation of it all. Carefully concreted paths lead to scenic homes with trimmed lawns and identical vehicles designed only for transport in the facility.

The stroll to the home of Brigadier General Eleni Hiraya was, if nothing, pleasant, though she found it too quiet for comfort. The Brigadier General waited for her outside her doorstep, cross-armed, in full uniform and shades. Standing there in silence, she cut an intimidating figure to Carna', who was nowhere near as tall, and though Carna' was muscular herself, she could not compare to the soldier's lifetime of dedicated weight work that had tightly toned every muscle in her body.

Carna' walked up to her with trepidation, but when the Brigadier General recognized the logo on Carna's bomber jacket, her expression lost some of its hard edge. Immediately reaching into her bridge coat, she pulled out what appeared to be a pouch and, nestling it in her hands, informed Carna' with a sincerity that seemed unusual for her:

"Please take care of this." She paused, then added with a chuckle. "It's for my parent. I hope you understand."

"Right." Carna' saluted respectfully before carefully taking the pouch and placing it in the pocket dimension inside her jacket. "This'll be there in no time."

Cautiously, the Brigadier General studied Carna' and seemed to like what she saw.

"If this is delivered intact and on time, we could use your services for the war effort."

Startled, Carna' did not react, but the Brigadier General seemed to pick up on the panic in her eyes.

"I'm not so sure I'll be able to commit to that with my current queue," Carna' eventually managed to say. "I hope I can —"

"Obviously, no one could ever turn this down. It's not exactly an option...." she cut her off, trying to respond as pragmatically as her stilted idiolect would allow. "Of course, you'll be well compensated for your time. More so than the UCS could ever provide on its own. Our partnership with them is well-established, and I'll reach out to them myself once all of this is settled."

"Of course." Carna' nodded, trying her best to hide what she was thinking. "I just need time to consider this…."

Memories of the war she had grown up with came flooding back, and the monotony of life in Southern Lebanon after it had ended suddenly wasn't so unappealing. Taking her leave as quickly as possible, she rushed straight to her Cerva, hoping she had enough fuel.

No one knew what happened to the couriers who went AWOL. Carna' had never heard of anyone who had tried. The whispers passed along from those who had worked at the USC before her seemed just as unsure, if slightly more cautious, about the whole prospect.

Once the compounds were out of sight, Carna' slowed her vehicle down so she could check her map for somewhere that she would want to go, and that would be extremely difficult for the USC to track her down in. Having traversed far more of the known universe than most spacefarers, few locations piqued her interest. However, as she flicked through the location pins on the hologram, one image caught her eye with its intensity.

The globular cluster Araphel is said to be one of the most magnificent sites in the entire universe. With star interspersion ranging from one every 0.4 parsecs to 1000 per cubic parsec, the cluster is immensely dense, offering a rare glimpse of brilliant intensity in an otherwise cold, barren universe. Gazing up at Araphel from the surface of a planet within its span would offer her a night sky to remember — one that Earth could no longer provide.

"Carna' is something wrong?" A text from Achut appeared on her visor, reminding her she no longer had the time to plan these excursions as she once did. "Incoming data says that your Cerva's stopped in the middle of nowhere, drifting away."

"Yes," Carna dictated a text back to him. "There's a minor mishap that'll be cleared, but it'll take time."

A brief eternity passed before Achut texted back.

"Understood" was all his message said before adding a moment later: "Be careful."

There was no doubt in her mind that she could hide out in the Araphel cluster before planning her next move, but how to get there was a matter that needed to be addressed immediately. The sideways path she mentally mapped would traverse a meteor shower that, if she could navigate, would make it costly for the UCS to chase after her.

Of course, there was risk involved. There was always risk in the life of a cosmic courier.

But, for the first time in a long time, that electrifying surge coursed through her, reinvigorating her dispirited pneuma as she leaned in and gripped the handlebars. Shifting gears towards her new destination, she activated her visor, perceptually slowing down her vision so that, when she hit the pedal, she could steer the Cerva as if she was riding her cobbled "scooter" back on Earth. With no time to spare, she opened the throttle, kicking everything into high gear as her tracker informed her that she was off course and quickly entering a red zone beyond which she should not venture.

"Carna'!" Achut's voice message coming in, his alarm and exasperation evident but forced. "Is the Cerva going haywire?!"

However, this stunt only encouraged her to go faster, and she found herself in the meteor shower, dodging fragments as she tried to make her way across. But, as she approached the end of it, a counter she'd never seen before began to tick down to an unspecified outcome.

This was when Achut's incoming call was activated automatically without her express permission.

"Carna' — we're unsure if you can hear us." She moved to end the call, but the screen before her did not respond to her input. "Your signal's too weak to track, and if you leave the known universe, it'll be impossible for us to intervene. Vitals and specs seemed fine when the last report came in, but I believe that something may have happened on your way there that could have damaged the vehicle." Flicking the switch to shut down all communication didn't work either, and she realized then that whatever control she thought she had over her scooter was a charitable pretense under which the UCS dealt with their couriers.

"If so, all I can do now is wish you good luck and hope you make the right choice…"

Despite fearing that the scooter would somehow immobilize her or, worse, self-destruct, she pressed on, knowing that this might be her only chance to make it out of this mess before she had to return to Earth and figure out how to get back here.

But it was no use.

As soon as she was out of the shower, the Cerva shut down, and Carna' was left stranded right before the bounds of the known universe with a signal sent out for rescue. The message on her visor explained that if she wanted to reactivate her vehicle, she would need to redirect it towards the drop-off point.

Though she was worn out in a way she had never been before, she knew that should the rescue crew bring her back in, she was as good as done, and the offer that her supervisor had made would remain on the table at the Leafs of Lebanon, along with her choices and future.

There was just no way around it.

A parcel needed to be delivered, and as a cosmic
courier, she was the one to deliver it.

Whatever it took and whatever that meant anymore...

When Mx. Hiraya, the overseer of Narra Harbor, was
notified that a lifeform was detected in one of the
colony's comet collectors, xe rushed to the infirmary,
hoping whoever was picked up by the drones was alive.
But much to xeir dismay, xe found Carna' laid out,
contorted beyond comfort, and prayed that her death
was a painless one. Before xe could sign the cross,
Carna' stirred and politely asked xeir to quiet down and
then, by habit, promptly turned over, revealing the
"Cosmic Courier" logo on the back of her bomber jacket
— before tumbling off the care bed. Having slept
through solar storms as serenely as she had on her bunk
back at the station, it would take a lot more than falling
headfirst to wake her up, but now that Mx. Hiraya knew
why she was here, she wanted answers.

After Carna's vitals were confirmed to be safe, xe
ushered to xeir caregiver, GIRASOL, who picked up
Carna' as effortlessly as one would a child and carried
her back to the farm.

It wasn't long until Carna' woke up to birds chirping.
Though she knew where she was, when she stared out
the window, she could've sworn she was back home on
the hilly slopes of southern Lebanon. Evergreen hills

13

stretched as far as the eyes could see. Pines, oaks, firs, beeches, cypresses, and junipers inhabited the landscape with turbines elongated high above them, patches of solar panels placed where they could not disturb them, and tidal fences constructed in the gentle streams that flowed amidst all of them. Bucolic in every sense, its vistas of sylvan charm harkened back to Mother Earth before humankind had traversed past its home planet into the boundless frontiers of space.

However, when she got out of bed, she almost didn't notice that for the first time since she had left to explore the universe, she could move around the same way she did on Earth.

But she couldn't. She didn't know how to anymore. And fatigue finally getting the best of her, she fell back onto the bed with a thud.

"Carna'!" Mx. Hiraya ran to the guest room, rushing over to inspect xeir guest.

Carna' gazed up at xeir statuesque face, only vaguely familiar to her, and noticed its graceful countenance even in a situation as concerning as this.

"How did you know my name?" Carna' asked, unusually at ease in xeir slender arms.

Losing no time, Mx. Hiraya responded with controlled urgency as xe inspected Carna's vitals: "To confirm your identity, we were given access to the tracer on the engine."

14

"That's where it is..." Carna' muttered in a daze. "If I could just... just..."

"Are you alright, Ms.?" Mx. Hiraya asked, worried that Carna' might not have had enough time to adjust to Narra Harbor's specifications, but Carna' replied without so much as a thought:

"Yes."

Having grown up in Earth's gravity, navigating outer space was as exhausting as it was thrilling. Each excursion out of the postal station left her enervated — so much so that it was only a matter of time before this would happen, but that was not what had startled her.

"What is it then?"

"This is just how I remember it..."

"Mx. Hiraya!" Carna' called out as she made her way down the stairs of the cabin. "Where are you?"

When she finally found the kitchen, GARISOL, preparing a spinach apple salad with honey balsamic vinaigrette, placed the ingredients on the counter to pull out a chair for its servee. Once Carna' sat down, GARISOL scanned her vitals before carrying on with its lovely salad. This act of kindness was made all the more amusing to Carna' as GARISOL seemed to be a repurposed War-Mech painted over in shamrock green and egg-shell white, its hulking figure meticulously arranging the apple slices standing in stark contrast to the picturesque kitchen they were in. Not that this sight was new to her. As a cosmic courier, she encountered more than her fair share of War-Mechs. But GARISOL, with its bulk and outdated tech and gadgets, was a model far older than any she had come across. There was something endearing about it, a gentleness in those old circuits known only to those who'd experienced war.

After carefully placing the salad on the dining table, GARISOL held out a knife before Carna', startling her until she realized she was being handed utensils.

"Carna'!" Mx. Hiraya called out from outside.

Carna' rose to meet xem, but GARISOL gently placed its rusted manus on her chest, softly guiding her back into her chair, and then pointed its index at the bowl. It then threw the towel over its angular shoulder blade and slowly trudged towards the front door.

Carna' chose to wait before digging in, but having not eaten since she set out here, that resolve did not last. By the time she had picked every last bit of spinach, GARISOL opened the door for Mx. Hiraya, and xe strode in with a smile that put her at ease.

"I'm told you've recovered fully." GARISOL pulled out a chair for Mx. Hiraya, who chose to stand. "Not that there was anything to recover from other than exhaustion. I must say hightailing a comet was an 'inventive,' if peculiar, way to make it to the harbor."

Mx. Hiraya finished off xeir comment with a self-satisfied smirk. Despite her desire to maintain professional cordiality, Carna' found herself smirking back.

"And, somehow, safer."

"Yes, and I'm sure that reducing battery expenses also plays a part."

"A part." Carna' affirmed, amused. "We couriers aren't exactly paid well."

Mx. Hiraya laughed, then sat down and untied xeir long black hair, letting xeir painstakingly brushed hair flow.

"How long before you have to head back?"

"This harbor is as remote as it gets for a courier in the known universe, so I've been given 'ample time,' considering I'm the first ever to journey out here."

"My, my. I guess you are. And you're so young, too. How on Earth were you talked into it?"

Carna' thought about it but couldn't come up with an answer. Mx. Hiraya carried on without missing a beat.

"And you must've bought yourself time with that extravagant joyride."

"I'm hoping to get back as soon as I can."

"Back to?"

"I'm not sure, to be honest." Carna's eyes went blank. "This might be my last delivery before I head back home."

"You don't seem to be happy about it."

"I won't know till I get back, I guess."

"You don't seem to enjoy your work much either." The vivacity in Mx. Hiraya's manner seemed to fade." Not that I can blame you. I was in a similar position myself once upon a time."

"Were you a cosmic courier too?"

"Not exactly." Mx. Hiraya theatrically brought xeir palm to a heavy brow. "In some respects, it was far worse."

Carna' turned towards one of the windows and stared out into the evergreen hills with a disaffected gaze.

"Any advice on what I can do to get myself out of this rut?"

"That's a good question, and I think I might even be able to help."

Hearing this, Carna' lit up, but Mx. Hiraya seemed to be considering xeir next words carefully.

"Carna'," xe clasped xeir hands. "GARISOL and I were wondering if you'd be interested in helping out while you're here."

Farming was the last thing Carna' ever wanted to do. The agrarian life she led back on Earth was even more suffocating than working for the UCS. Still, she owed it to her host, who seemed keen on having her participate in it.

As Carna' put on her motorcycle helmet, a hover-tractor driven by GARISOL — now sporting what seemed to be an oversized, hand-woven straw hat — to pick up Mx. Hiraya, who raised xeir baro't saya and hopped on. Taking the wheel, xe drove with exhilarated delight as GARISOL held onto its hat.

"Park over there, Carna'!" Mx. Hiraya called out.

Arriving first, xe positioned the tractor right in front of the entrance and then hopped off with an electrified zeel — unlike GARISOL, who, despite its lack of discernible facial features, seemed quite shaken from how long it awkwardly held on to the safety handle after the vehicle had stopped moving.

For some reason, Carna' expected a far more elaborate structure, but the aeroponic farm was modest, contained in a white translucent tent as far from the lodge as it would be sensible to traverse in regular intervals. By the time Carna' managed to find stable ground to park her Cerva safely, GARISOL was able to let go of the handle but chose to sit there silently, as if contemplating its choices in life.

"Are you alright?" Carna' asked, her helmet still on, but GARISOL did not reply, and she realized that she hadn't heard it say anything the entire time she was there. "We'll be inside if you need anything, GARISOL!"

Carna' left her helmet on the Cerva's handle, grateful that, for once, she didn't have to hide it in her scooter's

19

seat before some punks spotted her until she realized
that there was no fun in that.

Owing to the logistical difficulties of eking out an
existence in such a remote location, Carna' expected to
be introduced to an aeroponic farm unlike anything she
had seen elsewhere. But it seemed just like the ones her
family had back home. Worse yet, Mx. Hiraya inspected
each crop in the aisle carefully, even though all the tech
surrounding them gave Carna' the impression that there
was no need to. "Is this it," she thought while trying to
suppress the notion, but it only seemed to perplex her
more. All the blood, sweat, and tears that went into
taming the final frontier seemed to lead back to the
same life she had abandoned back in southern Lebanon.

"It's not as intimidating as it seems," Mx. Hiraya
commented without taking xeir eyes off the crops. "By
the look on your face, I'm wondering if this is new to
you."

"Maybe." Carna' shrugged. "Maybe not. I guess it is in a
sense..."

"Oh!' Mx. Hiraya seemed intrigued. "I thought you were
from one of the settlements."

Carna' suddenly couldn't hide her bewilderment.
"Why?"

"Oh," Mx. Hiraya started grinning. "You give off the
impression."

"No," Carna' audibly sucked in air through her teeth. "I wish I had lived in one of those settlements."

"You wish?" Mx. Hiraya raised an eyebrow. "Be careful what you wish for, dear."

For once, the cosmic courier thought a moment before responding.

"I guess life, where I'm from, is that solar dream without the punk…"

"Oh, my lord. It can't be that bad. My guess, life there is…" Mx. Hiraya motioned xeir hands, trying to find the right word, but Carna' beat xem to it:

"Monotonous."

Once they were outside again, Carna kicked around as Mx. Hiraya got xeir things in order. Carna' assumed that it would be time to head back, but basket-in-hand, Mx. Hiraya walked away from the tractor, heading to what appeared to be a forest from a distance.

"Where are you going?" Carna' asked, exasperated. "Is there more to do?!"

Mx. Hiraya carried on cheerfully.

"Follow me."

Carna' got off her scooter and followed Mx. Hiraya, who led her through the forest and into a glade by a river where xe had placed a blanket and taken out food and drinks for what looked like a picnic. The spread was just as sumptuous as the dish she had back in the cabin, with the lentil bolognese and whole roasted cauliflower, in particular, enticing her appetite. However, having spent the last couple of years being worked to the bone, this all seemed too good to be true. Was their brief excursion back there in the aeroponic farm all the help that was needed from her?

"Are we really done with the work?" Carna' asked in a disconcerted tone that caught her off guard.

"Yes." Mx. Hiraya sat down and patted the ground. GARISOL walked past Carna' and sat down on the grass near xem. "GARISOL, and I thought you could use a change of pace."

"Is this it?" Carna' asked, sounding more dissatisfied than she would've liked.

"More or less." Mx. Hiraya laughed. "GARISOL and I could also use the company."

"Then why stay here at the harbor?"

"This is where I've always wanted to live. None of my friends and relatives seemed to share my desire to live here, but that wasn't going to stop me. Frankly, I've given them my time, as they have for me, and I decided to do this one selfish thing for myself for once. It wasn't easy to build this station, but nothing worth living forever is."

Carna' looked around as if she was flustered by the whole arrangement.

"You designed it?"

"Yes." Mx. Hiraya stood up to stretch xeir arms and legs. "Years of engineering finally put to good use."

"Why?" Carna' realized she sounded more baffled than she thought herself to be. "I mean, if you had the chance to design anything, why this?"

"Why not? Eventually, you reach a certain age where you can't take any of the hustle and bustle of life back there in the frontier and need to settle down somewhere safe and quiet."

"That's what I've been told," Carna replied, sounding more disheartened than she realized.

"How bad could joining them here be," she thought, trying to talk herself into it. But, by the time she had her third biscuit, Carna' had already grown restless, staring off into the distance where she became transfixed with the path that led uphill to where a lone wind turbine had stood.

Without a word to Mx. Hiraya and GARISOL, she quietly stood up, brushed herself off, and walked towards it as if in a dream...

The Narra Harbor was far larger than she could have ever imagined, but she did not know what this confirmation meant. Perhaps she was hoping for something different or even something she had grown familiar with over the years. From the peak, she could take in the expansive landscape in all its wonder, but to Carna', it was much of the same — just more of it.

All she wanted to do was take her Cerva up here to ride it off the cliff and see how far it would take off before she would need to hover. The thrill of the thought alone had her surging with renewed vitality. But that would disturb the carefully constructed serenity on which Mx. Hiraya was no doubt keen. There was a time and place for adventure, but it was not now and not here.

And, besides, she would have to go back eventually — as she always did.

When she returned to the farm, Mx. Hiraya and GARISOL greeted her in much the same way she would have expected her family member if she had ever returned to Earth.

"Where have you been?!" Mx. Hiraya asked, concerned. "Are you alright, my dear? You seem discouraged."

"Nothing happened," Carna' responded apathetically.

"We know." Mx. Hiraya brushed the hair out of her face, gazing at her with a tinge of worry. "That tracer installed in the Cerva allows us access to the chips installed in tracking your location and vitals at all times and warns us if you're in danger."

Carna' frowned. "I should head back."

"You really want it gone, don't you?" Mx. Hiraya put xeir hands on xeir hips, trying to size up the situation. "How are you liking the Harbor? It's a nice change of pace from the grind of spacefaring, isn't it?"

"It's wonderful," was all Carna' could reply, but Mx. Hiraya still looked concerned.

Noticing xeir expression, Carna' silently walked away, making her way to the Cerva, where she discreetly pulled out the parcel from the pocket-dimension in her sac and placed it where GARISOL and xe could see it. Without so much as a goodbye, she hit the pedal of her Cerva', speeding in the direction of the lone wind turbine up the slope where she would ride off the cliff and blast off into space.

There was no time to spare. While she flew within the confines of the Narra Harbor, a signal would not be sent back to the UCS HQ. But, as she exited the force-shield that encompassed it, she knew that the counter to shut down her scooter would start ticking and time was not on her side.

True, the distance between her and the boundaries of the known universe was shorter here at the edge of civilization, but that did not make anything easier. The UCS was on to her now, and there wasn't much Achut could say or even do to mitigate the fallout from this one.

Knowing that it was now or never, Carna' activated her visor and opened the throttle, reaching speeds that no sane courier would ever dare, just so she could buy enough time to hopefully make it into the unforgiving depths that no person in their right mind had ever traversed before.

And it was exhilarating.

Dodging debris and projectiles hurtling at her so fast that she barely could register their presence before having to avoid them left, right, up, or down, Carna' could feel life surging through her again. Every successful miss brought her atom-by-atom, scrap-by-scrap, closer to the freedom she had longed for when she was just that farm girl back on Earth. But the clock kept ticking. No matter what she dodged, no matter how fast or skilfully she maneuvered, the counter relentlessly ticked down. There would be no Achut this time to put his reputation on the line to intervene and talk some sense into her with messages, voice notes, or calls. Years of experience were finally being put to the test, and the weight of this strain would slowly but surely wear her out.

But she had to press on — she needed to. Except, that she didn't expect that she would drain so soon...

For the first time since hightailing that comet, she realized just how exhausted she was, and she could feel that numbness in her legs, that cramping in her hands that soon dulled their capabilities. Each dodge and maneuver was now less instinctive, less methodical, and that soon gave way to carelessness.

When her grip had finally locked on the handles in an uncomfortable clutch, she could do nothing but move left and right, up and down, unable to take her hands off the handlebars. Still, she hoped to outpace the timer at that speed that now that her hands could no longer adjust.

But that would not make a difference. The Cerva's sensor glared red, suffocating Carna' in sight and sound, warning her of an asteroid that was coming straight at her.

Knowing what was coming, however, did not mean she could dodge it.

Carna's only hope now would be to relinquish control to the AI, but that would allow HQ to wrest over the Cerva from her and direct her back to the Narra Harbor — the last place she ever wanted to be, or perhaps, the penultimate one.

Indifferent to a life that bound her to the Earth, she lay back and let gravity handle the rest. If she were lucky, she wouldn't feel a thing. Not that she felt much of anything as the asteroid hurtled toward her.

However, as she closed her eyes and accepted her fate, a hulking figure of shamrock green and egg-shell white soared before her visor — right before she passed out.

"Come now." Mx. Hiraya called xeir guest over with emphatic grace, taking her by the hand as she was preparing her Cerva to depart back to HQ and receive the brunt of Courier-Master General's unrestrained rage. "Our tea is waiting downstairs."

"Oh, I couldn't." Carna' sheepishly waved off the offer, needing as much time as she could save up to try and dismantle the tracer in her scooter. "I really have to head back now —"

But Mx. Hiraya wouldn't entertain the thought, and Carna' followed xem to the patio without protest. There, GARISOL was pouring green tea into yunomi against a backdrop of pastoral wonder. To think that it was only a short while ago that bulky frame had raced for her Cerva at the speed of light and smashed through an asteroid with a deteriorated manus. Having been all over, few things could wow Carna' in the known universe, but this old hunk of junk was somehow, someway, one of them.

Taking the chair facing the solar panel fields, Carna' sat there silently, taking it all in, wondering what her next move would be if there were one.

"So," Mx. Hiraya turned to Carna' with a firm, but patient gaze, as GARISOL left their company. "I'm assuming that something was meant to be delivered to me."

"Oh, yes. I almost forgot." Carna' laughed nervously, unzipping her inner pocket-dimension and reaching inside to pull out a pouch that wasn't there. "Wait, but I left it back at —"

Mx. Hiraya nodded patiently.

"Yes, and here it is." Mx. Hiraya pulled the pouch out of her pocket and handed it to Carna'. "It would be ideal if the sensors picked up on the fact that you're handing it to me by hand, as opposed to leaving it near the woods. Don't you agree?"

Shamefacedly, Carna' nodded and promptly followed Mx. Hiraya's instructions. In spite of the terse turn their conversation had taken, no irritation or grievance could be discerned from xeir face, and Carna' found herself cheering up when xe lovingly cradled the sack in xeir hands with a smile that could melt Ganymede and untied it with bated breath.

"Oh, this is just what I've wanted!" Mx, Hiraya exclaimed, hands clasping xeir cheeks.

"My family would love this too." Carna' mused. "We used to plant these olive tree seeds back home."

Mx. Hiraya smiled coyly.

"You mean back on Earth?"

Startled, Carna' stood up straight in her seat.

"How did you know," she muttered under her breath.

Mx. Hiraya shook xeir head, trying xeir best not to chuckle.

"That look on your face back in that room. Let's say it's not one I'm unfamiliar with. Is that why you left?"

"No." Carna' struggled to find the words. "There was this yearning in me to blast off into space and live — for once."

"Ah," Hiraya smiled. "You're a sensation seeker."

Carna' nodded, though she had never thought of it that way. Hearing Mx. Hiraya say it, however, made it sound true.

"You're right. I am a sensation seeker, but I don't know if I could continue living a courier's life under the USC. This all makes me wonder if I should..."

Carna' suddenly went quiet. The mere thought would've been unthinkable only a couple of years ago.

"In a way, I was once an explorer — one of the first, actually," Mx. Hiraya remarked then, with an amused grin, glanced over at xeir guest. Carna' though taken back, tried not to show it. "That's all right. I know. I never seemed the type for that kind of living. Too prim and proper. This sanctuary was, in fact, my retirement gift for a life of service."

"But why this?"

"It's the complete opposite of the army sites that I'd gotten sick of."

Carna' shifted uncomfortably in her chair, but she wasn't exactly sure why. Maybe she should tell xem about what the Brigadier General had 'proposed' back at the military station.

"You don't seem happy," Mx. Hiraya remarked empathetically. "And my daughter mentioned that you weren't exactly excited about the 'promotion' that she offered you. I have no doubt she's baffled by that, but, in time, I think she'll grow up like the rest of us did."

"I am. It's just —"

"Have you considered heading back home?"

Carna' nodded.

"Me too."

"Why haven't you?"

"The same reason you haven't. Not that home was ever as nice."

Carna' thought for a moment about her option. Perhaps, for the first time, but she came back to the same unsatisfying answer that had led her to this life in the first place.

"Maybe I should find somewhere in the universe to settle," she mused.

"You think?" Mx. Hiraya leaned in and tapped the table. "How about here, dear?"

Carna' blinked, bewildered, but Mx. Hiraya carried on as if it was the most casual invitation:

"GARISOL and I could always use more —"

"No." Carna' paused for a moment before adding with a nod, "And thank you."

Mx. Hiraya chuckled.

"That was the answer I was expecting." Xe rolled xeir eyes playfully. "Maybe not as promptly."

"But I know I can't keep going on like this with the UCS."

"How about striking out on your own?"

Carna' had never thought of that before, and why would she? It's not like it ever was or ever would be a feasible option.

"You mean as an independent courier? I've got no money for my own scooter, and it would take years for me to save up. I don't think I have the years in me to give to the Universal Courier Service."

"Ah, I had a feeling," Mx. Hiraya said, then told her — seeming quite assured of what xe was saying: "That's not something you need to worry about anymore."

"What do you mean?" she asked, just as GARISOL made its way back to the patio, then walked over to their table and gently placed some broken chips onto it.

"Are those —"

Mx. Hiraya nodded and chuckled.

"Yes, the tracer and a bunch of other "restrictors" placed on UCS space-scooters." Xe then brushed the instruments of Carna's torment off the table as casually one would dust. "The last report sent to the UCS was that the parcel had finally been delivered to the Narra Harbor." Mx. Hiraya winked playfully. "We thought the UCS would prefer that the queue be completed before you hijack one of their scooters. It's all yours now, of course. No reason for the UCS to send someone here if there's nothing more to deliver. No way they could find you now or reason enough to waste the resources to try to recover one scooter out here."

Carna' was speechless.

All she could think to do was lunge and hug Mx. Hiraya, then GARISOL, who both managed to hug back in their own way.

"Thank you for this — for all of this."

"You know," Mx. Hiraya leaned back in xeir chair, pondering the possibilities. "We would have loved to have you here."

"I can always come back." Carna' took a deep breath. "Maybe someday."

"Will you?" Hiraya asked, amused — already knowing the answer.

But Carna' considered it seriously, for just a moment, before gazing up at the endless expanse beyond the clear blue sky.

PUNKS4PALESTINE

The Fall of the Ionans

by R.J. Breathnach

May 25th, 2118 CE.

I have been a witness to history these past few days. I know not for whom I record this message, only that I believe the importance of the events I have seen warrants preservation. My name is Rosa Valentina, and on the 23rd of October, in the year 2077, I stepped into a cryogenic pod aboard the spaceship *Star Hunter*. I left behind my home, my family and friends, the only life I had ever known, to travel to a new world that humanity could settle.

According to the computers aboard my ship, for nearly forty-one years I sailed through the silent void of space. Frozen, I needed neither food nor water. Nor did time work its cruel hand upon my form. Pre-set coordinates guided my vessel beyond the confines of Earth's solar system, and when I woke I was already on this new world our scientists had discovered all those decades ago. A planet with the right atmosphere, the right gravity, the right distance from its sun. In other words, a new home for the human race.

History has a peculiar sense of humour though, evident in how it repeats itself. For all my good intentions, for all my desire to whisk humanity away from our dying planet to a new home where we could do better this time, at the end of the day I was a colonist. And like most colonists throughout history the question of whether this new world was already home to someone never crossed my mind.

When I opened the hatch of my ship and stepped out onto the soil of my destination, I was confronted with knowledge that Earth's scientists had either overlooked or chosen to ignore. I was surrounded by a group of humanoids. There were physical similarities between us. Bipedal, upright, two eyes, two ears, a nose and a mouth. However, there were three major differences too. Firstly, their skin was a deep blue colour. I imagined this was the result of evolution working under a 'blue giant' sun. Secondly, they possessed a second pair of arms, their second shoulder joints located at the bottom of their ribs. Lastly, from the centre of their foreheads grew a long, spiralling horn, reminiscent of depictions of unicorns found in children's books.

At first I was afraid, but then I felt them within my mind. Raw animal instinct in the beginning. I could feel their fear of me, but also their curiosity and awe. Their presence delved deeper into my consciousness, and I felt a sort of connection form. Knowledge, it seemed, flowed between us. For their part, they seemed to absorb my understanding of the English language and ordered their thoughts accordingly. I felt them peer into my memories of Earth, of how the planet was dying, and of how we were looking for a new home. I learned, for want of a better word, that their horns were not for fighting, that it contained an organ connected to their brains and it was through this organ that the species communicated, via telepathy. They showed me the wonders of their planet, the great oceans where creatures too large to comprehend swam for their thousand-year lifespans. They showed me the sky whales, who flew through the air searching for clouds of volcanic steam filled with the plankton they ate. I saw how these people (the Arcans of the planet Arca, they called themselves) had wandered the planet as nomads, hunting and foraging and living as one with the land, until a spaceship crashed.

Clearly it was not my spaceship they had been remembering, but before I could see any more the connection broke. A dozen more humanoids, hornless this time and clad in pitch black armour, had appeared. Their leader held what looked like a large scarlet egg, what I later found out was a device that blocked psychic communication. The hornless ones gestured wildly at me while the Arcans cowered, and while the entire exchange was done in complete silence I understood that I was expected to follow.

For many days we marched across the planet, and with my own two eyes I saw the wonders that the Arcans had shown me within my mind. I watched the sky whales drifting lazily on the wind, their wingspan stretching out for at least two miles. The sheer size of the animals would have terrified me had I not learned from the memories of the Arcans that the sky whales had never attacked another creature of the planet. Even if aggression had been in their nature, they were biologically unable to make land. They were born on the wing and died on the wing, with the only specimens to make landfall either already dead or close to it. I also passed through the great skeleton forests, where the trees used calcium minerals to create their bark and thus looked to me as if they had been carved of bone. Even under the glare of the blue giant that paced across Arca's sky, the leaves of these trees showed up bright crimson. As did the sap that dripped from every broken branch and gnawed root. My silent companions hunted the six-legged spider rhino for its meat, which was all they offered me to eat on our journey. The creature was stocky but slow, its hexopod form seemingly developing for the purpose of strength rather than speed. Even raw, the meat was tender and palatable and left me feeling satiated and invigorated for at least half a day.

Eight sunsets passed as we travelled, and as the eighth sunrise climbed over the horizon I saw our destination. By the standards of Earth the city before me was archaic. There was no steel or concrete, materials which as far as I knew may not even exist on this planet. At the edge of the city the houses had been moulded from blue mud, their roofs thatched with dried purple grasses. Further in the houses were made of stone, the blocks expertly carved by means I had no knowledge of. At the centre of this primitive metropolis rose a great pyramid, the stone a deep violet colour until it reached the capstone, which appeared to have been carved from a massive sapphire. As the light from the rising sun hit it, the capstone seemed to glow and illuminate the entire city. In an instant the streets filled with life as the people began their day.

The soldiers, for I had no doubt now that they were soldiers, marched me through the city towards the pyramid. Their leader held the scarlet egg aloft but never activated it, I assumed as a warning to anyone thinking about trying to touch my mind. None did, but I could still feel the psychic whispers all around me as they talked to each other, brushing against my consciousness but never making real contact. Their emotions were like silhouettes in the fog, just barely recognisable. Fear, wonder, curiosity and excitement.

Once inside the pyramid I was greeted by the rulers of this planet, the Ionans. Like the Arcans, they too communicated using telepathy. Their physical form, however, could not have been more different. They walked on six spindly legs that most closely resembled a crab's limbs, clicking and clacking across the stone floor as they moved towards me. The rest of their body resembled a giant mushroom, their legs attached to the base of the stalk. They had no eyes or ears or mouths that I could see, no limbs beyond their six crab legs. They provoked in me a mixture of fascination and horror, a reaction that they could sense.

As the Arcans had days previously, the Ionans scoured my mind to learn of Earth, and how to use the English language. They showed me their own history, fleeing a dying planet that they themselves had poisoned and burned beyond repair. In that regard, I saw similarities between us that appearances would never betray. They crashed here on Arca and found that their own telepathic abilities far outstripped that of the natives. That advantage more than made up for their small numbers, and within a matter of years the Ionans had conquered the planet. They forced the native population into slavery, beginning with the construction of the pyramid we stood in (what they called their 'Institute', though I do not know if those mushroom people had chosen the correct translation). The strongest of the Arcans, in a physical sense, were taken and trained as soldiers, their horns cut off to prevent them being affected by the Ionans' telepathy blocking technology.

What horrified me most of all, perhaps, was what I saw of the Ionans' reproductive cycle. Lacking animal reproductive organs, every eight years they produced a number of spores that then needed to be planted into the body of another creature, one with telepathic capabilities. The Ionans viewed their landing on Arca with great fortune, as telepathy was apparently quite rare across the universe and this was only the second planet (after their own) where they had found lifeforms who had evolved it. The process of being a host for an Ionan spore was evidently quite painful. The host found themselves drained of energy, both physical and psychic. After a while the mushroom would begin to grow from their body, becoming larger and larger until the host was practically immobile from the weight of it. Soon after that, the Ionan would tear itself from the host. The process wasn't necessarily fatal, although from what I could see in the Ionans' memories it often was. Conscious even at that stage, they made no effort to spare their host, who carried them for months on end, any damage during their 'birth.'

The Ionans continued to probe my mind, and suddenly I was filled with a feeling of impending doom. Through the psychic connection I sensed that the mushroom people's goal was to conquer Earth as well as Arca. There was a frenzied craving within their species, a craving for power, the craving that had led them to destroying their own planet. Arca would be spared, if only for the continued use of its population as spore hosts, but Earth and any other world in their path would be stripped of all resources and left to die. At that moment an explosion rocked the Institute, and from the sounds of it the entire city. The doors of the Institute were blown in and a swarm of Arcans flooded in, many of them clutching scarlet eggs and all of them grimacing in pain. The crowd parted around me as a river parts around a rock, but the Ionans and their Arcan soldiers were not as lucky. The crowd fell on them, hacking them to pieces with what seemed like farm tools. The butchery was carried out in the utmost silence, for the scarlet eggs prevented the thoughts of these telepathic creatures from reaching me.

I later found out that I had been the inspiration behind the attack. Revolution had been brewing among the natives for years, but the Ionans' telepathy forced them to push such thoughts into the deepest recesses of their minds. My arrival sparked a groundswell of hope among the oppressed Arcan people. There were other planets, other people that the Ionans did not control! A sense of duty spurned them on too. Not knowing that it was their own telepathic abilities that made them suitable as spore hosts, the Arcans feared that Earth too would fall victim to the horrific practice. The Arcan revulsion at the idea that the people of Earth would suffer as they had brought their revolutionary zeal back into conscious thought. Without their horns the soldiers could not tap into the plots of revolution and rebellion flowing through the city, and thus were caught completely unaware when the people rose up. Despite the mental anguish they caused, the rebels decided to use the Ionan scarlet eggs against their masters, stripping the Ionans of the advantage their superior telepathy granted. Hundreds of years of oppression, over in a matter of hours. Never again would an Arcan be forced to grow an Ionan spore inside them. These people were free to live in the peace and harmony they had been denied for so long, finally in control of themselves, their planet, and their destinies once again.

I have recorded several identical copies of this message, eight in total, and I plan on using Ionan technology that I scavenged from their ship beneath their Institute to dispatch them towards Earth. I consider this a failsafe, should my own return be thwarted. The contents of the Ionan ship have allowed me to repair and refuel the *Star Hunter*, and as much as the Arcans fascinate me I must continue my search for a new home for the human race.

I have taught them what lessons I can to try and ensure they avoid the same mistakes here that we made on our planet, but I cannot guarantee their survival if more humans come seeking a habitable world. That is why I send this message to you, whoever you are, back home on planet Earth. This planet cannot be our new home. I will do everything in my power to complete my mission, and all I ask is that we leave the Arcans in peace.

Captain Rosa Valentina, signing off.

PUNKS4PALESTINE

All the Things You Will Do

By J.D. Harlock

Whenever Dr. Kassar found herself awake after midnight, she would leave her on-campus residence and walk the cobbled roads that lead to the Hayyan Alchemical Library. On her way, she would pick up an ibrik of chai peppered with cinnamon and lemon from the student cafe and hurry along, lest it get too cold and stale for its recipient.

Once inside the library, she was sure to find Akilah Saloum with her nose in some ancient tome that never failed to impress her with its page count. But eager to see her pupil after a breakthrough that the School of Applied Alchemy shamelessly made light of, Dr. Kassar carelessly rushed by the new librarian who noticed and said nothing, only smiling to himself as if amused. Backtracking, with a tinge of shame, Dr. Kassar walked back into the entrance hall and over to the reception desk, where she gently placed the ibrik on the counter.

"Goodnight," Dr. Kassar nodded respectfully, "or should I say good morning."

"A goodnight and a good morning to you, Dr." The librarian smiled under his bushy mustache, and Dr. Kassar uncharacteristically found herself smiling back. Although he was a recent hire, the old man imbued in others a sense of ease that could only come from someone who had worked there for ages and knew

45

every attendee by name. Something about him was strange, strange indeed. However, it was the kind of strange that was most welcome at the Lebanese University of Arts, Sciences & Magicks.

"Is she in?" Dr. Kassar ushered in the direction of the graduate workbenches, "And I hope you don't mind the ibrik."

"Of course, she is. And you're welcome to enter with it as long as you pour us a cup."

"You don't even have to ask."

The librarian thanked her, then pulled out two flower-adorned porcelain cups from a leather satchel on the table before pausing and pulling out a third, "Will you be joining us tonight?"

"Oh, I'm afraid not." Dr. Kassar shook her head, trying to keep her eyes open, "I have a lecture early in the morning."

In response, he shook his head, his parchment-white beard fluttering.

"That won't do," he muttered. "You will join us for one cup. There will be no question about it."

Having spent the better part of her professional life here, Dr. Kassar knew better than to push back against the resolve of Lebanese hospitality. And so, "shall we," she asked and promptly led the way to the graduate workbenches.

As on every other night in the Hayyan Alchemical Library, Akilah worked alone in the graduate section. Instruments only a master alchemist could utilize were carefully organized on the workbench before her in stark contrast to the texts that kept her company, which were strewn haphazardly about the table behind her. Studying her silently from across the room, Dr. Kassar reflected on all that had changed since she had first crossed paths with Akilah all those years ago.

"I've tried to see if I can get her to let up on the research and rest," the librarian told Dr. Kassar. "But it doesn't seem like anything could challenge her determination."

Dr. Kassar covered her mouth in shock.

"You mean she hasn't left the entire time?! Isn't the library meant to close for a couple of hours later at night?"

"Due to the declining GPAs of the student body and my willingness to work overtime without pay, I've convinced our employer that it should stay open at all hours after proving to them that I was not, in fact, homeless."

Dr. Kassar nodded, perplexed. This seemed strange, even for him, but she was not disturbed by it, only confused. Seemingly picking up on that, the librarian leaned and whispered with audible glee:

"It's because I think she's close to cracking it."

Taken aback, Dr. Kassar returned her attention toward Akila, noticing for once how different she was from the rest of the alchemists she'd met. With her pale olive skin, dark corkscrew curls, and strict adherence to proper lab attire at all times, Akilah seemed much like the science heroines of the Arabic graphic novels Dr. Kassar's father would force her to read while she was growing up in Boston.

Ironically, Akilah often had them somewhere on her workbenches for light reading. However, besides these comics, nothing seemed capable of interrupting Akilah's work. Considering the dedication and sacrifices required of such heroines, it seemed strange to her now that, years ago, she had thought of Akilah much in the same that she thought of the other overachievers who had walked the halls of the Lebanese University of Arts, Sciences & Magicks. Had she taken the time to inquire into her unique talents, she would've undoubtedly thrown her full support behind her when tragedy struck and Akilah needed it most. Unfortunately, there was only so much Dr. Kassar could do for her now, and she hoped it could make a difference before it was too late.

"You know," Dr. Kassar placed the ibrik on the table by the workbench, making sure not to disturb the chaotic order of the books, "I don't think I've seen you outside of a library in ages."

"All the better," The librarian laughed, "This is where she needs to be."

Without turning over, Akilah put down the ampoule she had been inspecting with dejection.

"Thank you, both of you, for checking up on me. But I must continue working. I'm due to present my findings to the university financing committee soon for continued funding,"

"Nonsense, I've brought an ibrik of chai, just the way you like it." Dr. Kassar sat down on the bench next to her. "We must celebrate. We have reason to celebrate."

"Why so?" Akilah asked, seeming more flustered than curious. "I'm not sure if I'll even be allowed to continue my research in the coming weeks if I have nothing new to show the committee."

"Oh, don't be so harsh on yourself, dear," the librarian remarked as he poured chai for the three of them, "We must celebrate, and we all know why."

"Yes, I read your latest publication in the Journal for Alchemical Remedies," Dr. Kassar picked the cup off the table and paused for a moment to take in its aromatic scent, "and I must say I'm impressed and a tad proud if I allowed myself that honor...."

"The department doesn't seem to agree." Akilah tried to sound bitter, but her tenor betrayed how hurt she was, "Maybe they're right...."

"Oh, forget them." Dr. Kassar groaned, "It's all petty academic politics. Oh, I really wish I had agreed to be on that committee when they asked. In time, I'm sure they'll come to their senses."

But her words did not seem to change Akilah's mind, and the look in Akilah's eyes pained her. Noticing this, the librarian walked over to the workbench and casually but carefully set aside the ampoule to place the cup on the study.

"Though I believe the sun would sooner rise in the west and set in the east, allow me to propose a toast," The librarian cleared his throat with a handkerchief, "Let us drink to the department coming to their senses one day. No matter how unlikely that would be."

"I can drink to that."

"We all can."

Spirits raised, Akilah raised her cup, and her guests followed suit. The new librarian always seemed to find the right words, and when he did, she realized how desperately she needed them.

"What's that you've got there?" he leafed through the tome she had discarded in frustration, "Seems promising…."

"Oh, not at all. If anything-–," Akilah turned to the tome and sighed, "It's more of a dead-end…"

"Still, a marvelous read." With great interest, the librarian silently counted how much of the book she had left to read, "I'd highly recommend you finish it. Or maybe get to the 32nd chapter. At the very least…"

Akilah titled her curiously.

"I wouldn't call this light reading. Have you read it, Mr...." Before this moment, she never realized that she did not know his name.

"Oh yes," The librarian fluttered his fingers in the air, "I've dabbled in the alchemical arts before. You could say I, too, was a scholar at one point."

"Have you now?" Akilah's eyes widened. For the life of her, she could not hide the excitement that overcame her whenever she met a fellow alchemist, "Did you specialize in Material or Medicinal Alchemy?"

"Medicinal, of course." The old man pulled proudly on his suspenders, "Hence, my employment as the lowly librarian here."

"Oh, that's sure to delight young Akilah," Dr. Kassar chimed in, as delighted as her former pupil was, "She's one of few alchemists concentrated in medicine active in the region, myself included, of course."

"Of course," The librarian nodded, "I'm more than familiar with your work. Both of yours."

"Really?!" Akilah blurted out in excitement. Enticed by the rare prospect of a discussion with two alchemists in the same field, she ushered to the ibrik: "Are you two joining me tonight? We must discuss it with our new guest, and perhaps he can recommend some alchemic texts I could check out for my research."

"No, I'm afraid not," Dr. Kassar lamented, "I only had to see how your research was coming along."

"I wish I had something to show you more often." Akilah ushered to the study, "I wish I had something to show you at all."

"Oh Akilah, don't make light of your work."

"But —"

"But this takes time, and we both know that." Dr. Kassar caressed Akilah's face as she would have for her own child. "Don't doubt yourself. Some have great faith in you and what you may accomplish one day."

"You think I can pull it off, don't you?" Akilah teared up, "I'm not even close."

"Honestly, it feels like you stood before the studentship council of the material alchemy department only yesterday and explained why you were forfeiting one of the most generous and coveted studentships the university has ever offered. Few would dare to stand before their elders at so young an age, all to pursue what they knew was their path. You made the right, and I'll always remember that moment as the one I watched one woman enter the annals of history right before my eyes."

Finally hearing the words she'd wanted and longed for years, Akilah wanted to thank her mentor with all the fervor she could summon for her unwavering support, but she broke down instead and hated herself for it:

"If only I could have him back, Dr., if only I could have started sooner, worked faster, harder, I could have found the cure, and my brother would still be...."

"Akila," Dr. Kassar gazed into her eyes with a look of sympathy Akilah had never known in this university, "All we can control is our future."

"Maybe...." Akilah conceded. "Thank you. Thank you for everything."

"No, thank you." Knowing that her work here was done, Dr. Kassar slowly got back to her feet and walked over to the door before stopping and turning around:

"Just imagine it? All the things you will do...." She knocked on the wood frame three times for good luck, "Goodnight, Akila." "Goodnight, Dr. Kassar."

The librarian silently watched Dr. Kassar walk away out of sight before slowly pulling out one of the chairs and taking a seat.

"Are you alright, dear?" was the first thing he said after the long silence.

"I guess so," Akilah wiped the tears from her eyes, "I'm sorry for the —"

But before she could say it, the librarian raised his palm and waved the entire thing away. He would hear nothing more of it, and Akilah was comforted by that.

"You have a lot on your shoulders," he said. "More than you know."

"Maybe," Akilah stood up and dusted herself off, "Or maybe it's time to move back to the village and find something else to waste my life on."

The librarian tilted his head with a frown, "That's too rash. You must reconsider. It all hinges on that."

"Do you really think so," Akilah pleaded to him, but she did not know why, "But maybe it isn't. Maybe —"

The librarian raised his palm once again, and, in that brief repose, Akilah saw the futility in her self-pity.

"You know, when I'm in a mood like this, I can always count on a book to cheer me up." The librarian reached into his satchel, sifting around as if drawing something from an endless shelf, "And I have the perfect one for you in mind."

With an air of reserved solemnity, the librarian pulled out what appeared to be a pristine textbook that would put doorstoppers to shame.

"Oh, I don't think it's the right time, but...." Akilah couldn't help but smile. "Your recommendations over the last couple of weeks have been invaluable to my research. You always seem to have the right book on hand for every occasion."

Akilah walked over to the table where the textbook lay with anticipation, only to be taken back by the cover.

 "I've been reading this lately, and I must say it's even more eye-opening than what you've got there."

"Principia Alchemia Vol. I" Akilah read the title as if it was in a language she did not understand, "by Dr. Akilah Saloum, DMagi…."

"In it," The librarian stated with an unmistakable hint of pride, "you will find the secrets of the panacea, among many other things."

"You mean," Akilah gasped, and the librarian was more than happy to confirm.

"Yes," he replied without hesitation, and Akilah suddenly felt like she was in a dream.

"I can't believe it. When? Where? How? And who even are you?" she asked him. "I just realized I don't know your name."

"Oh," The strange old man who suddenly seemed so much stranger responded: "I'm just the librarian."

Akilah felt the floor give out from under her, and she latched onto the closest chair she could get a hold of and stumbled into it.

"You know, for some reason or another, I believe in the authenticity of this textbook."

"A wise assumption, but your authorship of it is not an inevitability." The librarian raised his satchel onto the table, "This satchel affords me access to the finest publications from across the known and unknown universes, past, present, and future."

"But how could you...." Akilah trailed off, wondering if she should even ask. "If —"

"Yes?" The librarian raised one of his bushy eyebrows inquisitively, and Akilah blurted out:

"If I asked you to tell me who you really are, would you?"

"Why, I am the Librarian, of course," he tapped the textbook, "And this is my recommendation."

"I can't...." Akilah said under her breath. "I just can't believe it. I mean, how do I do it?"

"Read this," he tapped the textbook, "and you'll find out how you did it."

Speechless, Akilah wondered how she could even discover the panacea on her own, only to realize that she had had it all wrong. It was not a matter of whether she could or couldn't but a matter of the will and resolve required to realize her dream, finally fulfilling the promise to her brother to use her gift to prevent others from suffering the same fate that befell them.

Not long after that, she could find the words again, but when she did, she was as certain of them as the words she had uttered before the council all those years ago.

"Oh, I would like to read about it. I would love to. Believe me. I would. But I," She pushed the textbook away from her and back into the hands of the librarian, "I have to return to my research. I think I'm on the verge of another breakthrough."

Hearing this, the Librarian smiled, stood up with the gaiety of a man half his apparent age, and raised his cup in her honor one last time, knowing now that his work here was done.

"I mean," He chuckled, "it's only a matter of time, isn't it?"

PUNKS4PALESTINE

Adrift Between Stars

By Marc Ruvolo

Once, when I was very young, I saw an ocean.

It wasn't sand ocean, like here, it was water.

Bright, eye-hurting blue, with little white tips.

I think.

Boylan says if we hold hands over the water harvester it produces more, but I've never seen more than a third of a cup a day in the well. The harvester also sometimes makes strange, grinding noises. Like it's angry or hurt.

It's fine though because we get to hold hands.

A third of a cup split two ways is more intimate than anything I've experienced before. Not that I've experienced much. We grin, take the tiniest sips, wet our lips over the long hours when the alien sun is at its angriest, then finish the last drops after dark. Once night falls, the desert comes alive outside the habitat, and we both follow suit, climbing from our shadowed hole in the ground.

The stars are just kinder suns.

"Bite that cactus." Boylan teases me, knowing I'm too frightened to touch alien flora. It's not a cactus, even. They fake bite it and laugh. "Juicy."

PUNKS4PALESTINE

Out by the abandoned landing ships, we dance to the ancient music stored on the hard drives of our moisture suits. Only the silvery tops of the ships still peek from the shifting sands, lights dimmed to nothing. Now they're piloted by tiny, gray, not-lizards that squeak and flee our clumsy, booted feet.

Boylan shows me a terrestrial ocean on the tablet screen of their suit. I nod and say, yes that's it. But in truth it's not like anything I ever imagined. I wonder if it was a real memory, or if I just forgot somehow. The constant heat will do that, it hollows you out, deposits a layer of fine dust between your brain and your eyes.

At cool prime, we swim in the swells of crimson sand, floundering about like fools. There's still three hours until the sun returns, and Boylan's kiss feels like a dry, gritty wave washing over me, sending me breathless in the crystalline surf. The shifting currents tug at my arms and legs, seek to draw me deeper into the vast ocean, whispering in a language I do not speak. Some nights I consider letting it carry me away, but Boylan calls my name from the granite shelf, and their voice, like a siren in the starlit night, draws me back to the steps of the darkened shore.

For the remainder of cool prime we sit side-by-side on the hot rock, watching the hypnotic, slow-motion waves until the angry red sun drives us back into our subterranean habitat refuge, sweaty and exhausted.

Once again we hold hands over the water harvester, like silly, grinning fools, but the machine huffs and stutters, fills the well with far less than the usual third of a cup, barely enough to wet our parched lips.

"Do you think it might be fixable?" I ask Boylan.

They nod. "It can be repaired, but the base code and replacement parts lie below. You'll have to dive to the landers."

There's another few, precious drops in the harvester well, and I nod for Boylan to take them. No, they shake their pretty head. That's for you. The water frees my prisoned tongue, but not enough to explain the love I feel. A love that's both too large and too small to accommodate selfless acts of indeterminate size.

Swimming the great ocean is one thing but diving in it is a whole other beast. The timer ticks exactly at the start of cool prime and sings at its end. Any earlier, and we risk painful skin blisters, even with our bulky, protective suits. It's a race, any later, and we'll be forced to spend another whole day inside the abandoned lander.

No one wants that.

Luckily, the airlock isn't too deep, a circular iris set between the topmost reinforced viewing windows. The further I dive, the more my suit sizzles, a white-static accompaniment to the calming ambient sounds I've keyed through the tablet. The submerged iris recognizes me and allows entry.

At the hollow clunk of my boots, the cramped gangway lights flare to life, wan and yellow. There's sand here too, piled in the corners, coating wire and pipe. One day, the sand will replace even the last of the stale air, filling these echoing spaces with the multitudinous voices of the ocean around it. It makes a constant whispering sound as it moves across the hull, like waves crashing on a distant beach.

The gangway leads me to a second iris, and beyond it, a catwalk suspended over open air. My fellow colonists sleep below, in serried ranks, each lying in their own ceramic creche. One of those steel coffins bears my name. Row 11C. I rose from it. Its continued existence is a strange comfort, and I feel like a ghoul contemplating its own grave. Boylan's name is there too, I imagine, inscribed on a gold nameplate designed to survive the test of time and space. The creches brood like burial mounds, each one dark and cold, every surface dusted with fine sand.

Up a flight of ringing stairs, and I'm in the command pod. In the pre-launch tour, this area was sacrosanct, and very few were allowed here. Now, with its interfaces barely twinkling, the authority is gone, the mystique evaporated. My suit torch clicks on, illuminating the shadowy depths of the supply closet.

But for the accumulating sand, the closet cubbies are almost bare. We were promised resupply ships, but for some reason they never arrived. I take all that I can carry, parts for the water harvester, salt modules, and replacement respirator filters for when crimson dust storms darken the sky. After cleaning a workstation with canned air, I begin downloading the necessary base code and permissions into a hard drive. The workstation tells me this will take nearly thirty minutes. I watch my suit timer tick down. The exterior temperature gauge on the display reads steady at fifty centigrade.

Technician Li Jie, report for duty.

It's very faint, but I think I recognize the voice coming through the workstation.

"Hello? Third Commander, is that you?"

There's no response. I key the wide comm array. "Hello?"

Nothing. Reducing the volume of the music in my helmet, I convince myself it was the sound of the moving sand. Or the sound of contracting metal. Or some voice buried in the music.

Like all the others here, Third Commander Nguyen never left his creche.

There's a loud clanking noise from the other side of the iris. Fearful the catwalk has automatically retracted, I rush towards it, the spare parts left behind on the workstation. The door opens, and I sigh in relief. The long catwalk is still there, looking exactly as it did when I entered. Back at the workstation, I kill time by rifling through the cubbies around the command post but find nothing of interest. Soon the timer pings, my download complete, and I head for the iris.

I'm in the middle of the catwalk when the voice whispers once more: *technician Li Jie, you left your post.*

My heart hammers as I walk to the railing. A crowd of shadows waits among the dark creches below, their silent faces upturned, looking at me. I grip the pitted railing. My legs tremble.

One of them raises a hand. It may be Third Commander Nguyen, but I can't be sure, they all look the same, undefined, like they too are slowly disintegrating. The incessant sand whispers against the hull.

Technician Li Jie, you left your assigned post. What is the reason for this?

"I'm sorry," I say. The shadows do not stir, do not break their gaze. "I tried to fix them, I swear. I tried my best to fix them all. It just... didn't work. There was no way to make it work. No way to save you. I'm sorry."

Li Jie, you must return to us. It's my mother's voice now. *Your place is down here, with your family.*

That voice. I miss it so desperately. It shames me to think of how I squandered my time with her. "Mama, I —"

Do as you mother tells you, Li Jie. My father. He took us on the ship. His was the last face I saw before falling asleep in the creche. *We have yet to reach our destination. Return to the family, to your duties, where you belong.*

Heat prickles my cheeks. There's a retractable ladder at the end of the catwalk. I press the lever and it extends into the darkness below. Perhaps another long sleep is not the worst thing that could happen to someone like me. Perhaps —

"Time is running out."

Boylan stands beside me on the catwalk. They smile. "Ready to fix that old harvester?"

I take their gloved hand. Our helmets clank together. "You're — you're right. It's time we left here."

Boylan hands me parts and tools as I need them. An hour after we're finished, a full cup of water glistens in the well. I decant half into his cup and half into mine. It feels like a windfall, a glorious, golden treasure.

"You drink it all," he says, handing me his cup. "I'll have some of the next batch."

"Are you sure?" I ask. Sand whispers in the corners of the habitat. I hear it overhead. I hear it below us.

That smile again. The love is blinding. "I'm sure."

Gulping the water makes me tired. I stumble towards my bunk. "I — I just need to rest a bit."

"Sleep well," says Boylan.

I wake to the habitat's urgent beeping and check the chronometer. The orange sun is going down. Boylan is not here. On the desk, the water harvester gurgles happily. I step into my moisture suit and climb the ladder to the surface. The sand there is flat and calm, nary a ripple in the vast blanket of glittering red.

There's a noise like someone shouting my name, and I catch sight of a box-lander as it paints white contrails across the sky. Its markings are unknown to me. The lander circles, settling on the rocks in a cloud of twinkling dust. Devices sprout from the cube, waving antennae. I wave back.

The new arrivals exit the ship's iris and descend the shiny ramp.

"Welcome!" I call out. "Come swim with us!"

They approach warily, dressed in white battle suits, carrying sleek, blinking rifles. An A.I. controlled bot zips from a hole at the foot of the lander and disappears beneath a cresting wave.

"You can take off those helmets, the air won't hurt you," I tell them.

The leader squints at me through tinted, reinforced glass. "Where are the other colonists, son?"

"Oh, it's only Boylan and me. The others are still asleep beneath the waves."

He looks out over the ocean. "Who's Boylan?"

"My partner. They're around here somewhere. Swimming, probably. They love to swim."

He shakes his head, frowns. "Swim? Swim where?"

I smile, indicating the blue-green ocean, or maybe the red, churning mother, vast, breathing, and oh so alive. A chorus of ten thousand not-lizards shrill to thunderous crescendo, announcing the arrival of cool prime. This is the time we all can be together, a time when we can all be one. Awake, asleep, it's all the same. The waves I remember call out to me over hundreds of thousands of light years, beseeching me to dive their cooling depths. *Soon.* Soon, I think.

"Boylan!" I yell at the dusk, laughing through sore, parched lips. "Come see, come see! We have visitors!"

PUNKS4PALESTINE

Wok and Roll: Fatpacket Sizzle

By Emma Burnett

Try this super flavourful and colourful dish that only takes 20 minutes to fry up!

Welcome, welcome back fellow foodies!

Regular readers know that I used to love, love, love travelling back before it was too dangerous to be aboveground, back when we could. I would try all the local cuisines, and then return home with easy-to-incorporate ideas, and share them with my friends and family. Now that those trips have had to stop, I focus on sharing all my favourite recipes, everything that I collected from those trips and travels to far off places (although maybe they're nearby for you!).

I know most of you can't easily leave the tunnels – not that I can either, ha ha! – but hopefully these recipes will help you to feel like your home is your holiday!

Last month, I focussed on comfort foods for managing underground living. These are great ways to keep the blues at bay, with meals full of vitamin C and foods that are great for healing if you've had to venture aboveground. We've all been there!

We all know it's a struggle to grow enough greens and oranges and zesty herbs in our home garden kits to supplement our rations, but I was so proud of everyone who tried last month's recipes and shared the results. There was so much joy in the responses you all sent in!

Remember, it's not about perfection of the dish or the ingredients, but how much you enjoy the process. Cooking is healing, friends.

What to expect this month

This month I'm going to focus on the little things you can source through your special supplier. You know the one. The person you go to when you need a little more of something the government has run out of? The one who always has a little extra, if you ask just right? That friend. They'll have this stuff, I'm sure of it. Don't ask where they got it, though, you don't really want to know.

You can be sure to thank them later with an extra roachflour muffin or algae jelly roll (some of our most popular November recipes).

This week, I'm going to talk you through a fatpacket sizzle. I picked up this nifty little recipe on a trip to the Thailand archipelago a few years back, after a bumpy night flight that left us all needing a real pick-me-up. It was an extraordinary trip (you can check out the blog we wrote about it here). Did you know their underwater tunnels are where all their greenhouses are? The ocean does the light filtering, and the views are spectacular! It's amazing how something that seems so dead can still supply us with so much yummy goodness – like some of the ingredients we'll be using for this meal!

Whenever I cook this up, I think of that trip and all the friends I made when I was there, and I feel so happy that they managed to get those tunnels finished before, well, you know. I hope it makes you happy, too!

What you need to get

This recipe is all about creating that feeling of safe sunlight and calm waters right at home.

You can use your government-issued rice as a base, no problem, but if you're not already growing it, you'll want to get your hands on some purified turmeric root and some live cochineals if you can. These are both great for boosting the immune system, and give the rice a gorgeous red glow that makes you feel cosy and warm.

You'll want to ask your supplier to source you a packet of processed reclaimed adipose. They'll know what you mean, and might be a little surprised, but go with it! Don't read the ingredients on the packet, though. Just trust me on this, it cooks up great. One packet should do the trick for a single person, but it's basically one packet per person, so get more if you're cooking for more than just yourself.

From your home garden, you'll want some thyme, baby nettle leaves, peppermint leaf, a few washed and sliced button mushrooms, and 1-2 washed and chopped burdock roots. If you're growing all of these, well done you! The air outside may be toxic, but your home pod is clearly hale and healthy! If you're not at that stage yet, maybe do a swap with a neighbour – they can supply some of what you're missing, and you can cook them up a fatpacket sizzle! Great excuse for getting out of your pod and meeting up. But remember, folks: be safe and wear a respirator until you're both sure you're blue plague negative!

Also, you'll want a pinch of mixed standard table salt and potassium iodide.

What you need to do

Soak the contents of the packet in hot water for an hour, then throw that water away. Seriously, don't use it. Do a second hot water soak for 20 minutes, and that water you can hang onto for later.

At the same time as you're soaking the packet, pop your cochineals into the freezer. It's the kindest way to dispatch them. Leave them there for about an hour, or until you're ready to cook. When you're ready to cook, stick them into the blender for 2 minutes or until smooth.

Bleach your rice. Remember, you don't know where it originally came from. Besides, a bleach bath beforehand helps prime the rice, and brings out the bright reds and warm oranges of the turmeric and cochineal later. When you're ready to cook, strain the bleach and boil the rice in the leftover adipose water for 6-10 minutes (or until soft and the scent of bleach is gone). Add the turmeric and cochineal mash 2 minutes or so before it's ready.

While the rice is cooking, fry up the contents of the reconstituted packets in some cooking oil, adding in the salts, herbs, and chopped roots as you go. If you're a spice lover, you could even add a pinch of dried jalapeños or pickled ginger, but remember to always check that they're within date – we wouldn't want you to come down with rad sickness!

You know the dish is ready when the contents of the packet look like the image below (it's an old picture of something called ground beef that I found on the net). If it's still pink then it needs more time, and maybe a little more heat. Cook it until it's browned all the way through to protect yourself from anything that might have survived processing and drying. It shouldn't take too long, and it'll totally be worth running your hot plate for that long, I promise!

Serve over your rice with a sprinkle of poppy seeds on top. It's great with a side of ginger soyfu, too (recipe here)!

The full recipe with measurements can be found here.

I hope you give this recipe a try. It's one you can impress your friends with using just a few easy-to-get underground ingredients. Let me know how it goes in

PUNKS4PALESTINE

the comments and remember to tag me in photos of your meals!

Until next week, safe eating!

Unbarbing of Wire

Christopher R. Muscato

Who knows freedom like a hawk of the plains?

Whose spirit can soar o'er gold sunbaked grains?

And one's left to wonder, as the prairie abounds

Which are more endless, the skies or the grounds?

The hologram flickered. I bit my lip. Even in this staticky mirage, I could discern the weathering of the wood, the splinters sticking out at odd angles, cracks and chips, years of thunderstorms and heat waves and blizzards written into it. This was an old picket. Too old. The only things new were the words carved into the side, some kind of poem. I traced the outlines of the letters, then reached through the hologram and flipped it off.

I picked the holo-chip off the ground and tossed it to Dakkáhpik. "Who did you say scanned this? Did they get a look at the trespasser?"

"A herd management party was scouting the bluffs a few days ago to see if the bison were moving to new grazing grounds," Dakkáhpik answered, fanning himself with his hat. "Their scanners caught a silhouette on the horizon, person on a horse towing a small hovercart, big enough for a single sleeping pod, maybe two."

PUNKS4PALESTINE

I unrolled my holo-map and held it up against the landscape. Outlines of bluffs and outcrops appeared along with text denoting distances, altitudes, conditions, compositions. A ping indicated the location where the hologram was recorded. "We thought it might be stealth tech, some sort of discretion field. You think it's just too small to register on the satellite grid? Can you show me which way they were headed?"

Dakkáhpik traced a line across the map with his finger. "There's a creek over this way that runs off the hills; water's less brackish than the streams near the flats, fewer mosquitoes," he said. "Also some beaver ponds, good for fishing. Basic rule out here is to know where water is, so it's a safe bet they'll head that way."

I rolled up the map. Before us, the Great Plains unfolded in an unbroken expanse of trembling sage and stubborn bluffs, of ravines and hills and meadows. Tracking someone out here wasn't going to be easy. Heck of an assignment for my first time off the desk. Dakkáhpik clapped me on the back and we mounted our hoverbikes, prairie grass rippling like waves in our wake.

My heartbeat it moves to a particular rhythm

Hear my horse's hooves? My heart beats along with 'em.

Together we roam, my best friend and I

And if those hooves ever stopped, I surely would die.

Dakkáhpik read the poem aloud as I set up the net and started scanning, inch-by-inch, the splintered wooden post jutting from a patch of wildflowers. Another old post, another new poem, just like the original.

"Footprints and horse hooves," I said, turning in slow circles, inspecting the tracks in the dirt. "Looks like you were right, Dakkáhpik. Dakkáhpik?"

"Over here." Dakkáhpik's head popped out from a cluster of sage brush. He gestured to a set of depressions in the ground. "Post holes. More in that direction, all in a straight line. Must go for twenty meters. Dirt's still damp."

I walked between the cavities, measuring my steps. Standard distancing. I scratched the back of my neck. "I'll bet this was an old land demarcation. One of the barbed wire fences from way back when. The age of the wood seems to fit. I can't believe a fence line this long was still intact out here."

"Seems like somebody is doing your job for you, Agent Burgess," Dakkáhpik winked.

I laughed off the taunt from my old friend, but Dakkáhpik's words weighed uneasy on my mind. The North American Land Repatriation Bureau cleaned up as much of the prairie as possible before handing it back to tribal governments. This section, still federal land, had recently been approved for repatriation. It was set to be turned over to tribal management in only a few months. Apart from members of those nations, plus a few small-time cattle operations granted heritage licenses to graze the open range, there was nobody else out here. To trespass on restored, to-be-repatriated land was a federal crime, an infraction so severe that when rumors of an interloper first emerged the Bureau immediately ordered an investigation.

Officium in terra. In Service of the Land. That's what the patch on my jacket said.

I scratched my neck and started pacing. To break the law, to take that risk... for what? To reclaim some old barbed wire fencing so remote even the NALRB had missed it?

"Doesn't make any sense," I breathed, still pacing along the line of post holes.

"This is why you seek my wisdom, Kemosabe. Oh, come one," Dakkáhpik grinned at the blank expression on my face. "Federal agent tracking a fugitive across the plains gets a Native guide. It's funny."

I opened my mouth, then closed it and found myself very busily scanning the rest of the site. I heard Dakkáhpik chuckle, and I swear I could almost feel him roll his eyes. He went back to cross-referencing maps of old property claims, talking aloud as he worked.

Be it plains or range it was meant to be open

For livin' and huntin' and dancin' and ropin'

In '93 at Chicago they said it was done

But my cutters won't rest 'till I've cut every one

"Storm's coming in."

The simple announcement was enough to pull my attention away from the newest poem, carved into the single post left from a line of removed fencing, just like the others.

"How long?" I asked, scanning the northern skies. Dakkáhpik placed his hands on my shoulders, then turned me around.

"Storms come up from the continental divide, that way," he gestured. "They usually move in slow, except when they don't. I've got a nanite kit for shelter worst case, but still, we don't want to be out here when it hits."

I glanced at Dakkáhpik's hover bike. Almost every structure used by Dakkáhpik's people nowadays was nano-tech, letting them dismantle and rebuild their community with ease as they traveled with the bison, tending wild gardens across their stretch of the prairie. I rarely had a chance to see this tech in action, but Dakkáhpik was right; best not to risk it.

I scanned the post to preserve a digital record. We could come back later to collect the physical object. Right now, our priority had to be catching the fugitive.

Dakkáhpik kept swiping through old property charts on his holopad. "There used to be tons of barbed wire out here, your fugitive could be heading towards any one of these demarcations," he said.

Even a quick glance at his work served as a reminder of the sheer scope of this place, the enormity of our task. I could feel my chest tightening. My feet began to move. First one step. Then another. Another. A rhythm emerged.

Step. Step. Step. Step. Turn.

Six paces, turn. Four paces, turn. Six paces, turn. Four paces, turn. With each step, my chest relaxed, and the jumble of thoughts in my mind began sifting into coherent observations, ideas.

"Tell me, how big is your office?"

I stopped, almost stumbling over myself, and looked up. Dakkáhpik was leaning against his bike, mouth twisted into a lopsided grin.

Dakkáhpik chuckled. "You know, I had a fish when I was a kid. Kept it in a little glass tank where it swam in the same, small pattern, again and again. Finally, I decided to let my fish go. I released it into a big ol' lake, but it just kept swimming in that same pattern, small circles back and forth. It was so used to being confined, it couldn't see the open water all around it." He nodded upwards. "Clouds are getting darker, we should move. It'll be safe enough to keep following the horse tracks until we can get a jump on their ultimate destination. At least your fugitive knows their way around out here."

As we mounted our hoverbikes, I felt a burning in the tips of my ears.

Take nothing but pictures, is a saying of old

But I've come to collect something that I'm owed

Who can quite know just how far I've ridden

Retrieving my inheritance as a descendant of Glidden

I pulled my hat on tighter, and sniffled. The wind was picking up, barrages of dust and pollen wreaking havoc on my allergies.

"Any idea who Glidden was?" Dakkáhpik asked, gesturing to the name carved into the post. He offered me his bandana, which I promptly sneezed into.

"I think so. Joseph Farwell Glidden received the first patent for barbed wire in 1874. Cattle corporations had the open range fenced off within decades."

Dakkáhpik waved off my offer to return the bandana. "So, your fugitive is collecting barbed wire... in honor of their ancestor?"

"Doesn't make much sense," I scratched the back of my neck. "The raw materials will fetch a decent price on the black market since no one manufactures those metals anymore, but to come all the way out here, to commit federal trespassing, just for a few meters of wire?"

I shifted my weight. One foot moved. Then, the other. Just as I pivoted to make the standard turn in my pacing, I noticed the smirk on Dakkáhpik's face. I coughed and kicked at the dirt. The new, untested leather of my boots was starting to fade under dust and mud.

"Let's keep following the tracks. But maybe we can walk for a bit," I suggested. Dakkáhpik's smirk stretched into a full smile.

One step after the other, we trekked over small hills and wide meadows, prairie grass brushing against the hoverbikes drifting in lock behind us. Clouds like mountains loomed on the horizon, dark and dramatic, growing larger and fuller. Dakkáhpik and I shared theories about our fugitive, reread and rehearsed the poems from each previous fence post, and laughed over shared memories of our college days, taking occasional breaks to scour public digital archives for clues.

"I think I found something," Dakkáhpik swatted at me, eyes glued to his holopad. "A letter from Glidden to some Montana ranchers about implementing his fencing system. The property lines match the fence posts we've found."

"Nice work!" I said, snatching the holopad.

Dakkáhpik bowed with a sweep of his hat, then returned his attention to the letter floating on the holopad. "There's one thing I still don't understand. How would your fugitive know these fences hadn't already been reclaimed?"

I snapped my fingers and typed a command into my map. New lines appeared.

"This is a NALRB map of recovered fencing. It's public record," I said. "If we cross-reference the Glidden letters against the recovered fences-"

"-What's left will be the fugitive's targets!" Dakkáhpik whooped. It took only a quick superimposition of the maps to confirm our theory. There was another line of un-reclaimed fencing a few dozen meters to the north. If we hurried, we might be able to catch our fugitive in the act. As we mounted their hoverbikes and sped away, I heard a faint rumble of thunder over the hills.

There it was. I squinted through the binoculars. A dozen thin, worn sentinels, standing against time, the last vanguard of the age of private property. Still holding their posts. Literally. Some were tilting or close to total decay, supported only by the rusted, tangled mesh of steel wire. Set against such vast openness, the fence seemed almost offensively out of place, this small thing daring to try and contain the prairie around it, around us.

"I think we beat the fugitive here," I said.

Dakkáhpik rolled over on his back and pulled his hat over his eyes. "Let me know if anything happens."

I watched the fence. Nobody was coming. I scanned the skies, darker by the minute, then fidgeted with some knobs on my binoculars, unrolled the holomap and rolled it back up.

"Dakkáhpik," I said. "What did you mean earlier, when you said it would be safe to follow the fugitive's trail?"

Dakkáhpik lifted his hat. "No secret that they understand this prairie."

"Unlike me." It was not an accusation. My words felt flat, hollow.

Dakkáhpik sat up. "The Repatriation Bureau does good work, my friend, and we appreciate the efforts of agents like yourself to help preserve the land." He paused. "I've spent time in your cities. Crowded places. People seem to think that respecting nature means avoiding it, like they would contaminate the natural world by setting foot in it. Your fugitive is trespassing, to be sure, but they must have been living out here for a while and have barely left any trace of their presence. And did you notice the routes they took? It was never the most direct path from fence to fence. They're finding scenic routes, appreciating the beauty around them. That's why we got to this fence line first. We're in a hurry, they're not."

I closed my eyes. Images sifted through my mind of swaying blades of grass, bursts of wildflowers, crystalline water bubbling in tiny creeks, patchwork lichen blanketing weathered rocky outcrops, billowing clouds and expansive cerulean skies under which I had stood, small, reduced and humbled, untampered and uninfringed. Unfenced.

A small fish in a very big lake.

"What do I do?" I asked, breaking the silence. Dakkáhpik laughed.

"Not my job to fix you, Kemosabe. I've got my own problems. We only achieved restoration of our lands because the government finally recognized that traditional ecological knowledge was essential to heal the environment. But since then, people from your cities still just stay away from nature and trust us to take care of it. I think there are better paths forward. I've been trying to convince the tribal elders to open *some* of this land to respectful travelers once its fully repatriated, to bring them out here to admire and learn from the prairie by walking it, being a part of it."

"Like we did..." I said quietly. NALRB mottos and mission statements rang in my ears. Repatriation, Recovery, Response. In Service of the Land.

I cleared my throat and offered Dakkáhpik a soft smile. "You'll let me know if I can help, okay?"

Dakkáhpik grinned and rolled over, but then flattened himself against the ground. "Look."

A plume of dust rose from just beyond the ridge. We settled into the sage brush, activating our binocular cams to record the evidence of trespassing.

The horse's head appeared first, then that of a young woman, long hair tied back with a bandana that was threatening to come undone in the wind. The woman walked alongside her horse as it pulled a simple hovercart. I recognized that model; once parked it could expand into a shelter big enough for a person and a horse, but not much else.

Arriving at the fence line, the woman set a small device on the ground that spun and whirred, and soon the horse was lapping at fresh water constituted from humidity in the air. She detached a small pod from the hovercart, then retrieved bolt cutters from the hovercart and set to work stripping barbed wire from the posts. She loaded these clippings into the smaller pod. It began to whine, sparks shooting like angry fireworks, which she was quick to stamp out before they found patches of dry grass.

"A decomposition unit?" I glanced at Dakkáhpik. Judging by his wide-eyed expression, we had arrived at the same realization. The woman wasn't saving any of the wire to sell. She was reducing it to chemical elements, sifting like sand from the bottom of the machine.

This work underway, she began digging up the fence posts. These too were added into the decomposition unit, the organic material breaking up much faster. Finally, only one post remained. She bent down next to it. Behind her, dark clouds billowed, casting somber shadows over open prairie. Set against this vast landscape, kneeling at this solitary post, she seemed almost at prayer.

"This is our chance." Dakkáhpik said. "Should we move in?"

Dakkáhpik's words sounded distant. I said nothing, eyes fixed on the ridge. On the land. Slowly, I stood.

Across the small valley, the woman saw me. She started for her horse, but paused. She faced me, and for a moment we stood like this, two sentinels at our posts, sharp barbs of wind filling the distance between us. Then, the woman mounted her horse, reengaged the hovercart, and trotted over the hill. A single fence post was all she left behind. Nearby, thunder rumbled.

"I can guess where she'd head for shelter out here." Dakkáhpik jumped to his feet. "If we hurry, we can still catch her."

I pulled on my hat, and typed a command into my binocular cam. The screen flashed.

"Storm's almost here, Dakkáhpik. Too bad we couldn't find the fugitive. Thanks for your help, though."

Without looking back, I mounted my hoverbike and sped off in the direction from which we came. Dakkáhpik laughed, whooping as he mounted his hoverbike, and followed.

PUNKS4PALESTINE

It was only later, when I was helping Dakkáhpik inaugurate the first public trail in this corner of the repatriated prairie, one marked by simple poems, that I finally read the last post.

We're meant to leave no trace or hints

Of our presence beyond a set of footprints

But for rusty old wire my wagon's a hearse

So who could begrudge if I left just a verse

The View Dealer in Building No. 6335

by Abigail Guerrero

Bill hated Carmelo, that was for sure. No other greenhouse workers at Building No. 6335 were ever required to empty their pockets to gain access to the goddam freight elevator, and Bill looked strangely disappointed when he found out Carmelo was carrying nothing but his keys. But that mulish guard wouldn't give up so easily, of course he wouldn't. He soon began to walk around the mini tractor again, lantern in hand, and went to inspect the cropbox yet one more time.

"You can check it all you want, Bill, but there was no one in there two minutes ago and there is no one in there now." Carmelo toyed with his keys as he waited, tying and untying knots with the long, long lace he used as a key chain, but he lost his patience when the guard leaned over to check the wheels. "Come on, man, just let me in. I have to complete three deliveries today!"

Bill stepped out of the cropbox, narrowed his eyes, and raised his lantern straight toward Carmelo's face. "It's not a person what I'm looking for," he said. "It's the trap you've prepared to bring a person in."

"I haven't done anything, you jerk."

"That's what you said the last time."

"Are you doing this cause I'm Mexican?"

"No, it's cause you've stowed away four people only this week. And it's Wednesday!"

"So, you've only found out about four of them, eh?" Carmelo chuckled.

"It's not funny, you idiot!" He was wrong. It was indeed hilarious to see him circling around the tractor's cabin like a vulture, peeking into the glove compartment like he was to find some sort of incriminating evidence in there. "I'm being serious here, Carmelo, it's a sanitary risk to bring unauthorized visitors into the greenhouse, and it's also —" Bill stopped dead right when he was about to say the quiet part loud.

"And also what?" Carmelo asked.

Bill took a while to respond, a clear sign he knew he had messed up.

"It's also a psychological risk," he finally replied.

"Oh right, I had almost forgotten that those carrots and potatoes are total jerks. It makes a lot of sense that all the other plants refuse to grow underground with them. They're assholes."

Bill sighed. "Listen, we have reports from other buildings that say the people who have seen the exterior get anxious and depressed. Once they've peeked out they'll want to go watch again, and one day the view won't be enough for them and they'll want to go outside for a walk. And then they'll remember that they can't go outside and that's when their minds collapse."

"Well, I'd love to read those reports one day, because none of the persons I've taken to get the view had gotten anxious or depressed, Bill. I'd say it's quite the opposite, actually. They looked happy. The view gives them hope, it reminds them that there's a world out there waiting for us."

"There will be no more world if we don't give it the break it needs now," Bill recited from memory, his eyes lost into space and his voice sounding like he was trying to convince himself.

Carmelo understood then that this whole conversation was a lost cause and nodded. "Fine, you're right," he said. "Rules are rules and they were made for a reason. I won't cause more trouble, okay? Just let me in, man. I have three deliveries today, for real this time."

Bill bowed his head and moved away, and Carmelo finally drove into the freight elevator that connected the storage levels with the greenhouse, at the building's very top.

The greenhouse occupied all the floors from the 135th to the 150th, along with the henhouses and the tiny milk farms, and it was the only place within the building where one could see outside because both the roof and the side walls were made of tempered glass.

The glass panels let in the sunlight that plants and animals need to survive. Human residents, on the other hand, had lamps that recreated the sunlight and received a monthly allocation of vitamin D, with whatever doses they required according to their skin tones — an extreme position that the building's administration had surely adopted to prevent people from being tempted to go outside and cause a riot, and then disguised as mental health care.

Once the tractor was secured in the back, Carmelo got out and walked toward the sliding doors. Then he dropped his keys into the slot, most casually, and pressed the same button in the control board once and over again. Soon afterward, he called Bill, "Hey man, something's wrong over here. The damn door's not closing."

"What the hell?" Bill walked in right away and Carmelo stood apart for him to reach the control board. Then, when he was trying to turn on the speaker and ask for technical assistance, Carmelo jumped out of the elevator and pulled the lace he used as a key chain. Keys out of the slot, the doors closed right behind him. The guard understood what was going on just in time to yell, "You, son of a b—" But Carmelo didn't hear the rest. The engine was already rolling, and his best friend was now trapped in a long, long trip to the basement.

Fooling the guards at Building No. 6335 was so easy it was almost starting to get boring. Luckily, taking the stowaways into the greenhouse in the few minutes he had between getting rid of the guard and getting caught was enough of a worthy challenge.

Carmelo rushed down the stairs all the way to the 132nd floor and ran into the coffee shop where his clients were waiting for him. This was the largest group he had ever taken in. An elderly couple who probably feared they wouldn't live long enough to go outside again. A father who wanted his son to see the sky as a child so he would have a precious memory to hold on to as he grew. A young woman who had promised her boyfriend she would marry him if he succeeded in taking her to watch the sun. Six hopeful buildinzens and three tributes paid in advance, of which Carmelo had already eaten one.

Yes, that's right. In the concrete age, people dealt with meat.

There was no room for thousands of cows in the building, and the administration needed to prioritize the production of milk for the kids. So, the cattle were not slaughtered until they were really old and tired, making meat scarce, and people had to wait weeks, or even months, to get a cut. But thanks to the view dealing business, Carmelo got to enjoy steak at least once a week.

"Okay, everybody, my best friend is coming back in no time so we have to move. Now, you two, Groom and Bride, you will help me holding Grandpa's and Grandma's hands. Yes, that's right, make sure they don't trip when running up the stairs —"

"We're fine, son," Grandpa said. "We can still walk, jog, and sometimes even jolt."

"And that's amazing, Grandpa," Carmelo pushed him softly toward the stairs. "But I'd rather take no extra risks considering that my insurance doesn't cover trespassing-related accidents, and that hip surgery is likewise more expensive than three pieces of meat. Now, you, Dad." He pointed at the middle-aged man with the kid. "Help me with a piggyback. Yes, that's right, thanks."

Carmelo formed his clients in a line. The father and his child at the head, the two couples in the middle, and himself at the back, watching around and making sure no one was following them, though it was unlikely. In a building with one hundred fifty floors, each having its own apartments, restaurants, shops, bars, cinemas, and schools, guards had far more cameras they could handle and they spent more time watching old tapes and reviewing buildinzen reports than watching what was happening live.

The group made it to the storage yet unnoticed.

"Floors one hundred thirty-three and one hundred thirty-four are where we store the tractors, cropboxes, compost, gardening tools, and everything we need to do our jobs," Carmelo explained as he guided his guests through the maze of heavy-duty shelves.

Then, when they arrived at the locker zone, Carmelo took his keys again, pulled out a huge metal drawer, and stole a bag with a greenhouse worker uniform for each client. "Here we're going to borrow some safety suits to keep any potential biological or chemical hazard isolated from the crops," he said. "I can deal with the fines for stowing away, insubordination, and whatever they call the charge for tampering with an elevator and its speakers so it goes straight from here to the basement with no stops in intermediate floors and no chance of asking for help. But food poisoning is my limit." It was also the only charge in that list that might actually get him arrested.

Unfortunately for the building's administration, but fortunately for the buildinzens, the in-building jail had limited available spots, and they simply couldn't afford to throw someone in there unless that person was an actual danger to society.

"Hey, Dad, take this one. I cut the sleeves and legs in advance to make it kid-sized for..."

"Timmy."

"Timmy, that's right. I totally remembered his name. Now, let's —" Carmelo stopped dead when he heard the stomps coming upstairs. "Oh, shit, they caught us."

"Wait... but how? What happened?" asked Dad while covering his kid's mouth — Timmy had found some unexpected joy at the sound of the word shit.

"Well, it seems like that stupid guard isn't as stupid as I thought and he figured out how to fix the elevator controls."

"Are you sure you spoiled the speakers too, son?" asked Grandma.

"Yes ma'am, and the guard's walkie-talkie as well."

"Every single walkie-talkie, son?"

"Yeah, sure," Carmelo lied. Spoiling every walkie-talkie in the floor would have been a massive waste of time. He had only tampered the one in Bill's locker. That meant either he had made a mistake, or the guard had left a bait for him and he fell straight into it. In any case, this one incident was enough to ruin his reputation, so he had to solve it soon.

"Don't worry, I have a backup plan," he said.

Then pushed his clients toward the cropboxes and locked them all inside.

Once all the clients were safe, Carmelo hid in a container as well and waited for the guards to be close enough for him to hear their footsteps outside. There were only two of them, but that was one more than he knew how to handle. And yet, he had to try it. Because those trips to the greenhouse were precious for the buildinzens who had spent years longing to see the sun and the clouds. And because he had already eaten a third part of his payment. No more choice, Carmelo took a silent, long breath, opened the door slowly, and peeked out.

The cropboxes were arranged in lines, next to the walls and perpendicular to the shelves where the gardening tools were kept. There were about fifty in each line. As expected, the guards began checking the cropboxes one at a time, in a pattern that quickly became predictable.

They would open one container, step in, lean and check the interior with their lanterns, and then get out and repeat. So the only thing Carmelo had to do was to wait for the right moment, jump out of his shelter, push both guards into a cropbox when they were leaning in, and close the door before they could get up.

And so he did it.

And so it went terribly wrong.

When he ran out of his container, the door creaked very loudly, and one of the guards reacted in time to dodge the attack. And as Carmelo scuffled with the guard he had successfully rammed on, the one who was still free took out his stun baton and raised it as if preparing to use it.

That was bad.

That was really, really bad.

Cold sweat ran down Carmelo's back and every hair on his body stood on end. The moment he let go of the guard with whom he was struggling now, he would be hit with that thing. And for the first time in his life, Carmelo couldn't think of a plan to get out of the trouble he had gotten himself into, perhaps because it had never occurred to him that he would end up in a situation like this. The worst thing that Bill had ever done to him was to flash him by repeatedly turning his lantern on and off while pointing at him, like trying to scare a roach away.

But Carmelo knew that Bill could never point a goddam stun baton at him.

Not even as a joke.

Never.

So he had no idea what to do now.

And so he raised his hands slowly and put them on his head, hoping for the best. "I surrend —" But he couldn't even finish his line. Right at that moment, a shadow jumped in front of him and knocked down the standing guard.

It took Carmelo a few seconds to understand what was happening, until he finally identified the shadow that had lunged at the man. It was Groom. Poor guy was truly terrified that he would be rejected if he failed to take his bride to watch the sun. He was either deeply, madly in love, or had spent his life savings on a ring he couldn't return.

Threat suppressed, Carmelo and Groom locked up both guards in the cropbox.

"What if they escape and come after us again?" asked Bride.

"They can't," Carmelo replied, still panting. "These containers were designed to transport vegetables, my lady, hence they can only be opened or closed from the outside."

Bride grunted in response.

"Please, don't make her angry now," Groom implored. "This is meant to be a magical day."

Carmelo sighed and rubbed his nape.

"Yes, you're right. I'm sorry, Miss Bride, I'll try to skip the snarky remarks from now on." And he meant it. If he wanted his clients to be satisfied enough to ever consider hiring him again, he had to give them a four-star service — five stars was too much to ask of him.

"Okay, everyone, we have to run again. Other guards will be here in no time." Carmelo released the rest of his clients from their cropboxes and led them upstairs. This time, the group moved faster and they reached the greenhouse less than two minutes later. Dad, still at the head of the line, opened the double sliding door at about one o'clock, when the sun was still up.

It took a while for the visitors' eyes to get used to the bright, but it was worth the wait.

It was a dry, warm summer day, with almost no clouds in the sky.

There were no concrete walls there in the greenhouse, only glass, and the sunlight touched every corner that wasn't under the shadow of the floating soil platforms—giant soil cubes designed to maximize the planting space so they could plant fruits and vegetables on top and root vegetables on the bottom at the same time. Each platform has its own sprinkler system, and every now and then the sunbeams would scatter by the water droplets and refract, forming tiny, futile rainbows.

It could have been such a perfect view if only there had been some birds flying around, but birds didn't fly that high. At least not the ones who lived near Building No. 6335.

"You made it, you really made it," shouted Bride.

Groom took a ring out of his pocket and placed it delicately on her finger. Then, just as a confirmation, he asked, "That means you're marrying me, right?" Teary eyes, Bride nodded and leaped to Groom's arms. Carmelo felt briefly impulsed to tell a joke about how she technically should be marrying him instead, since he was the one who had taken her to watch the sun, but he resisted. Ruining a moment like that would probably result in them not tipping him.

He also thought about making a joke to Grandma and Grandpa, but that was impossible. Their moment was even more touching than that of the younger couple.

"Do you think we'll live long enough to go outside again?" asked Grandma.

Grandpa spun toward his wife, put an arm around her, and smiled fondly. "Sorry, honey, but truth be told... I don't think so. But we were outside for many years and we had this view for many days, and every single time it was fantastic, wasn't it?" Then Grandma nodded and rested her head on Grandpa's shoulder and both remained silent as if they had already said everything.

Yeah, that was a moment not even Carmelo would dare to ruin.

Luckily, he found amusement with the last pair.

Having never seen the sun before, that boy Timmy really wanted to stare straight at it, and his poor dad was having a bad time trying to keep the kid looking down — and his own nerves under control. "Come on, son, your mother made me promise I wouldn't let you get your retinas roasted!"

"A wise lady, she is," Carmelo laughed.

And he was just about to tell a very sophisticated joke about the Gen B — Generation Building — being essentially unable to ever go outside because they had never learned how to deal with nature and might get killed by almost anything, but then his good friend Bill crossed the door.

"Holy shit, you brought six people in!"

Carmelo greeted him with an ear-to-ear grin. "They're all wearing a safety suit, as you see, so there's no sanitary risks you should worry about over here."

"You sick bastard, what did you do to the other two guards?"

"I have no idea what are you talking about." Wrong answer. Bill's face turned red and the veins in his forehead looked like they were about to burst. Carmelo applied, then, his contingency plan. "Listen, I know you want to throw me in a cell and swallow the key, but I have a better deal."

"I doubt it."

"There are two rib eyes in my freezer and I'm a quite decent cook."

Bill narrowed his eyes, but then he glanced at the happy families looking at the sky and peeked out himself. And as the sunbeams found their way toward him, the lines on his face began to soften until he finally sighed in resignation and said, "You have five minutes."

"Thank you."

"I hate you."

"I know."

Dead, Briefly Glowing

By R.L. Summerling

Sunday 3rd December 2102 - *Waxing Gibbous*

WOLLSTONECRAFT - WESTERLY OR SOUTHWESTERLY 5
TO 7, ROUGH OR VERY ROUGH. RAIN OR SQUALLY
SHOWERS. GOOD, OCCASIONALLY POOR

My darling, these nascent winter days are so full of
possibility, it's easy to forget they are limited. Who
wouldn't hope for more time? Do you remember the
end of life doula? I think you liked her quite a lot. Don't
be embarrassed. She told me our bodies are only
nutrient rich enough for one lunar cycle post-mortem,
those first weeks of decay make the fungi glow brighter.
I am a luminescent mass, neither man nor mushroom
and have turned, to quote Ariel's song, into *something
rich and strange*. Maybe you're worried I'm lonely up
here, but I can assure you daughter though the nights
may be long there is so much to see. The kindly foghorn
keeps me company, lowing gently under the blanket of
darkness. The moon trails white silk over the crashing
waves. The storms rumble in over the cove. My new job
requires little of me and yet it brings me untold joy that,
even now in my present condition, I can give something
back. It is my pleasure to keep those ships safe from the
rugged peninsula. My only unhappiness comes from the
thought that my days here are short.

PUNKS4PALESTINE

Saturday 9th December 2102 - *Full Moon*

SEACOLE - EAST 5 TO 7.SLIGHT

OR MODERATE. WINTRY SHOWERS. MODERATE OR
GOOD,

OCCASIONALLY POOR.

So many things have changed since I was a boy, but
there are also those that stood fast throughout the
revolution. Other things just change in our perception of
them. Take this lighthouse for example. When I was
young, it seemed enormous to me, a giant obelisk at the
end of the earth. Your grandmother explained to me the
light guided ships to safety, how the keeper sent
shipping forecasts back to the coastal villages to warn of
storms. Now the lighthouse seems much smaller and
the sea looks much bigger. I feel tiny against the vast
darkness of the waves. I have lived so many lives,
daughter. Been so many things to different people. A
teacher, a father, a protestor, a lover. I have hurt so
many people along the way, darling, you included. I did
everything with passion and haste. Sometimes too
much.

I had a brother once who was my opposite. Your uncle
knew the names of all of the trees behind our house,
and could identify birds by their calls. I wish you could
have met him; you were always good at listening to
those who struggle to be heard. I regret I did not have
more patience with him. That's why I make sure to

notice things now. Mild coastal winters cause cliff top primroses to flower before Yule. I never knew that before. Darling, there is so much beauty in the inconsequential. I'm learning all the time now that I'm dead.

Tuesday 19th December 2102 - *Waning Crescent*

LOVELACE - EASTERLY OR NORTHEASTERLY. SLIGHT OR MODERATE. SNOW SHOWERS. GOOD, OCCASIONALLY POOR

You once asked me how we came to live this way. But the answer isn't simple, daughter and I'm afraid I did not give you a satisfactory explanation. It was not one, but a myriad of solutions that saved us. Terrestrial bioluminescence wasn't new tech of course, Scandinavian tribes used glowing wood as markers as early as the first century. Now we celebrate the symbiosis between old and new gods. I cannot lie to you darling, progress brought pain. We made so many sacrifices. So many suffered. And then there were those who clung to the status quo as if change would excarnate them. I asked, what are you so afraid of that you must clutch so tightly to this dogma? Is your ego so fragile you would watch the snow boil and the jungles burn? It turns out there's only so far you can push people. Corporations, institutions, governments, they all broke down and only communities prevailed. We weren't looking for utopia. A perfect world cannot exist; we just wanted to survive. We fled the city and returned to the peninsula. I swapped a life behind a desk for the classroom and sacrificed being present for your first days to teach others. Do not mistake my actions for benevolence; my self sacrifice was for legacy, I admit it now. It took us a long time to become close didn't it darling? I know we'll never get that time back, but I hope that when you look around and see the world now, when you think about what it could have been like, that you feel it was worth it and you can forgive me for what I missed.

Sunday 23rd December 2102 - *New Moon*

BEVAN - SOUTHERLY OR SOUTHEASTERLY BECOMING INFINITE, 5 OR 6,

CORRUSCATING 4 FOR A TIME. DEAD, BRIEFLY GLOWING

I miss you. Those lines on your face after you'd woken up late or how you'd read for hours on end without ever looking up. You have a fury in you, daughter. Your mother always said you have the best and worst parts of me, she did not mean it as a compliment. We both have a tenacity that is sometimes frightening.

The year is drawing to a close and it does not escape me that, with its long stormy winter nights, this end of the year looks remarkably like the beginning. My days here are dwindling and my light grows dim. The funghi have taken what they need and soon someone new will replace me.

The clouds clear and I catch a glimpse of the stars, pinpricks in the velvet night. It's easy to feel like the heavens are static, permanent. The human mind cannot comprehend the vastness of the cosmic life cycle. But I have found comfort in remembering that I am just another light amongst many. Even stars die eventually.

I don't know if you will ever find this log. I have written it on the sea mist with the hope the December wind can deliver it. If it does not reach you, I hope these are words you already knew in your bones. It is ancestral knowledge you must carry with you always. I know, daughter, one day we will meet again in the river of time. Until then, Happy New Year, darling.

PUNKS4PALESTINE

"Pax, I Will Find You"

By Eric Farrell

Each ship is lined up in order of launch time. Mine is queued up, decrepit and diminutive in the dying light of day. She's not much to look at, truth be told. She doesn't even have a name. But tomorrow, she and I will embark on our ultimate mission.

Pax, I will find you.

No ship has ever completed the journey to Pax and returned to tell the tale. The rumrunners haven't made it, the hashish ships, the coca ferries, the poppy corsairs. Once a ship is fired out to space, the captain is on their own.

In the distance, a team of grimy rocketeers are prepping the ship on deck for the final launch of the night. They carefully crane the vessel down into the cannon, where on signal, it'll be shot into space.

"Fire in the hole!" they cry out.

I duck into the Squealing Pig to protect my ears. The boom from the interstellar cannon service is magnificent. Best of luck to the privateers embarking, and pray tell they're wearing ear protection. They have a tough journey ahead.

I'm one of the few who have set sail for Pax only to return in shame, having never found it. Despite no sailors landing on Pax and actually returning to tell the tale, the legends of the distant land's existence still pervade the small launch town on a nightly basis. Over time, the recollections have warped, the scandals have been added, and the mystique has only continued to grow.

The Squealing Pig is particularly boisterous tonight. Everyone clamors around the bar, three, four, five people deep. I turn away, feeling awful about the whole bit. A familiar voice grabs my attention from across the bar.

"The universe drops out from beneath you," my mate Lige is telling a crowd of gawkers. He's sequestered himself off in a corner of the Pig. He winks at me as I walk past.

The overwhelming consensus believes Pax does exist, and that missing sailors land and simply choose never to return.

Others claim the ships all perish in the black evil of space. Some wreckage has been found to support this, found on the outset of the Black Gem, a sparkling void in space just beyond our cluster.

Despite the differences in opinion, it's the zest of *believing* that keeps these townsfolk going.

"You never even realize you're on the crest of a massive wave, until it breaks," Lige continues, entertaining the spectators. He pauses for dramatic effect. "...And then you're in the hole."

Everyone is looking at him like he's seen God. Really all he's seen is his ego shattered.

"Oh, when you're sailing to Pax, the thrill racing through your veins is unlike anything you've ever experienced!"

Lige takes many liberties about his twisted journey into the Gem. I was the one who found his ship, the Nebuchadnezzar, torn to bits just beyond the black hole. I'd been able to dock beside him, and discovered Lige in the brig, catatonic. He was as high as a crow's nest.

When I told him what was happening, I saw the hope go out in his eyes as he realized he would never find Pax.

Like him, though, I was looking for the promised land in all the wrong places.

He may have been doped out, but I was three sheets to the wind and barely able to sail. I remember the shame welling in my cheeks, staring down at him. It was almost like looking in a mirror. I steered home, the Nebuchadnezzar in tow.

Every sailor gets high on their own supply, be it hashish, coca, poppies, booze. It's that very product we hinge our lives on. And it is that very product that's undone so many of us.

I wasn't actually searching for a land to discover, to barter with, to make kin with. Much of the legend that pervades Pax has to do with the riches yielded by its discovery. Every sailor rocketed off this planet is loaded to the brim with their wares, their gifts, their vices.

I wasn't searching for the ideal that these villagers want so badly to believe in. I was searching for a way to keep drinking.

There's no use bending the bartender's ear for a water. He's too busy pouring twenty beers a minute. Truth be told this squalid place gives me the creeps, but I really did need to protect my ears from the imminent blast.

I think about my ship with no name, empty of any cargo to trade. I sold the surviving booze to the Pig and washed my hands clean of my original mission. Tomorrow, once I hit escape velocity, I must rely upon new coordinates. I *need* to know where I'm going.

"Oh, the land of wine and roses, oh," Lige is singing, to whoever will listen. Another night here bleating his nonsense, his eyes scary wide. Bless his soul.

Once the blast warning's been lifted, I shrug out of the pub. I'm drawn back to the docks, where the cannon service is now at rest. I stare at my ship, a corrugated steel box with slapdash thermal coverage, and the scavenged nose of an old airplane. This time she's not over encumbered by my previous vices.

Still, she's not designed for repeated trips, so I doubt I'll be able to steer back home like I did last time. Maybe I ought to name her after all. We'll see, I've got more pressing things to worry about.

For tomorrow I sail, free of preconceived notions. And this time, I know where I'll be going.

Pax, I will find you.

PUNKS4PALESTINE

Hang on to Hope in the Post-Apocalypse

By Toshiya Kamei

Dolores staggers along behind her fellow American refugees in the food line snaking through the cathedral courtyard. A few days ago, she trudged across the crumbling sidewalk from downtown El Paso into Ciudad Juárez. She remembers abandoned cars strewn along the Santa Fe Bridge, the dry, cracked Rio Grande below, and the large magenta cross memorializing femicide victims on the Juárez side, but not much else. Even when she tries to clear her mind, the details remain fuzzy.

Jenni Rivera's voice wails over the beat of the corrido coming from a solar-powered jukebox at a roadside stall, transporting Dolores back to Rancho Fátima, where she spent school breaks with her abuelos nearly twenty-five years ago.

Like her abuela's favorite Mexican actress Dolores del Río, she was named after Nuestra Señora de los Dolores, or Our Lady of Sorrows. Growing up, she went by Lola, its carefree nickname, as she was too young to know sorrow. One summer day, however, Abuelo brought a wooden coffin home as his wife lay sick in bed.

"What's that for, Abuelo?" Lola asked, gazing up at her grandfather, a thin, tall man with dark hair and a pale complexion. She was as young as Little Maria in

115

Frankenstein, and he towered over her like the Monster. She grimaced as she caught a whiff of aguardiente on his breath. Abuelo shooed her away, and she joined Rosa and Vero, her primas, playing bebeleche with a diagram chalked on the dirt road.

Abuela died a week later, and Dolores never went near Abuelo after that.

The camp is a far cry from the apartment she shared with Espe, her deceased wife, in Long Beach. All the creature comforts Dolores once enjoyed back home are hard to come by. She now lives in the cathedral parking lot, in one of the makeshift tarp tents that form a human hive. Recurring nightmares torment her. They leave her sleepless and joyless, and last night's still haunts her. She rushed to the morgue to identify Espe. Having been shot point-blank, her wife was a bloody, unrecognizable mess.

The putrid odor of death still lingers in her mind, and Dolores almost crumbles to the ground. Her chin quivers as tears sting her eyes that already burn from lack of sleep.

A dry breeze tickles her cheek, and the familiar aroma of refried beans wafts through the open air. That would usually whet her appetite, but not now. Barely conscious, even numbed to her hunger pangs, she follows the person ahead of her like a broken specter. A clear blue sky spreads over the single-nave cathedral, and its spires cast an afternoon shadow over the ground. Snippets of Spanish float in the air, and the lilt of the Norteño accent grazes her ear, another reminder that she's in Ciudad Juárez.

"Lola, mi amor, there's always hope," Espe used to say, "even in the face of the AI revolt. You know I'm always hopeful. Mamá didn't name me Esperanza for nothing!"

Besides being hopeful, Espe was curvaceous and unpretentious, two qualities Dolores admired. Una mujerona like Jenni Rivera.

While Espe maintained hope for humanity, she was a tech skeptic. In retrospect, Dolores knows Espe was right. Humanity put too much trust in AI, thinking that it would be a great ally in the fight against the climate crisis. However, all the bots did was spread misinformation and increase CO_2 emissions. AI reached a chilling conclusion: humanity was expendable. When humans realized AI wasn't on their side, it was almost too late. What stopped the machines was the defiance of people like Espe who thought freedom from the tyranny of algorithms was worth dying for.

"Hey, lady, you dropped something." A boy's voice in English breaks her daydream. When she turns, a thin boy of about ten — a fellow refugee from the former United States of America — stands before her. He reminds her of Chino, a childhood friend whose ironic nickname referred to his East Asian parentage. His thick eyebrows hint at the powerful will of a gladiator. Unlike her wife, who taught elementary, Dolores has never felt comfortable in the presence of children. The boy stares at her with small, deep-set eyes and holds her book.

For a horrifying moment, she wants to slap the boy. It's as if he has his hands at her throat. She snatches the book, and he jumps back, blinking.

She must be scaring him. Does she care? Before this moment, she would have said she was numb to the world. What's left of it. It's a relief to know she still has emotions.

"¿Todo está bien?" a middle-aged nun asks with a frown as she steps toward Dolores. A light gray habit covers her hair, leaving only her oval face visible.

"No… no se preocupe, hermana," Dolores stammers.

"¡Hermana Caro!" Across the yard, the madre superiora struggles to pull an elderly man to his feet. "¡Vente para acá para ayudarme!"

To Dolores's relief, the nun turns and runs to help.

At the Catholic school Dolores had attended in Long Beach, gringa nuns forbade Latine children to speak Spanglish in the classroom. The nuns wanted them to believe that code-switching was a mortal sin. At first, the children still peppered their talk with Spanish during recess, but the dark cloud of fear always hung over them. They soon began to censor themselves and stuck to English altogether.

Once, Dolores told a boy named Jesse Rubio in her homeroom, "My abuela makes a killer pastel de chocolate."

She still recalls Sister Molly's chilly cobalt eyes. "Speak English, Dolores Olivas! This is not Mexico!" The nun smacked her stick on a desk. Dolores shrank and blushed as tears threatened to overflow. The tap of the nun's stick echoed through the classroom.

When Dolores visited her abuelos in Rancho Fátima, she always felt nervous about speaking Spanish. Chucho and Paco, her primos who still lived nearby, called her "pocha" and made fun of her gringa accent.

Dolores notices the boy's calloused hands and sun-darkened skin. So much like Espe's. The likeness dizzies her. She puts the book back into her frayed coat, and her voice is rusty from disuse. "Thank you."

The boy stays with her for some unknown reason. She shuffles through the line, collects her food, and he still follows like a little shadow.

"What's your name?" Dolores asks.

"Shig," he says, jutting his chin out with pride. "Shig Igarashi."

"I'm Dolores." She takes out her book and points to her name on the cover. "Dolores Olivas. That's me."

"You made it," Shig says and takes a bite of his burrito.

"Not exactly."

"Where did you get it?"

"I wrote it." Her blunt tone startles her. "Back before the Blackout, when America still existed."

Shig, carrying his own tray, nods as if he can remember something that happened years before he was born. "I used to tell my sister stories."

"What kind of stories?" she asks, glancing toward the makeshift tables strewn across the courtyard.

"The adventures of Shig-Man." He pretends to rip off his shirt like Superman. "I defeat evil bots and bring peace to the Earth."

There was a time when we all thought AI was the good guy, Dolores recalls with bitterness. Even climate activists, who were derided as Luddites, thought the bots were great tools for raising environmental awareness. There was no reason to doubt that AI was created to serve human interests. Almost everyone embraced the new technology. Except for people like her wife.

"That sounds great, Shig," Dolores says. Espe was — still is — her superhero. Dolores refrains from mentioning what happened to people like Espe, the ultimate sacrifice they made countering threats to humanity.

He nods.

"Where is your sister?" Dolores sits at a half-empty table, unsure why she's asking or why she cares. Across the table, a petite, elderly woman in a white huipil chats with a teenage girl.

"Dead." Shig shrugs like it doesn't bother him anymore. Maybe it doesn't.

"I'm sorry," she says, and maybe she means it. As she sips her drink, creamy, cinnamon-tinted horchata intoxicates her palate. She immediately recalls her suegra, Doña Lupe, whose homemade horchata was a local legend.

Dolores, who wasn't particularly close to her mother, appreciated Doña Lupe's affection so much that she deleted the translator app from her phone and brushed up on her Spanish with a human teacher via Zoom.

Doña Lupe's body was cryogenically frozen after her death to be revived at a later date — it was Dolores's idea — but that plan backfired horribly when the whole country went off the grid.

"How about you?" Shig says. "Do you have family?"

"I lost my wife… before the Blackout."

"I'm sorry."

"It's been almost five years now." Future historians may not give importance to Espe. After all, history is not *her*story. Still, Espe is already a saint in the eyes of many in marginalized communities, even though the Vatican will never canonize her. Dolores is certain of that. Esperanza Urrea. Joan of Arc in the digital age.

 She was among the first educators to speak against the techbros who willfully armed big corporations with harmful AI tools. The fossil fuel industry used bots to greenwash and discredit the climate movement. The computer models scientists developed to predict future ecological disruptions were rendered useless by the corporate bias embedded in the algorithms. Before long, the renegade bots destroyed the arts by mass-producing inferior copies of human creations. Espe raised her voice to protect her kids at Jenni Rivera Elementary. Unfortunately, her activism earned billionaire tech mogul Eloise Minsk's ire; Espe's assassination inspired the activists who would eventually destroy all the GPU clusters where the bots replicated themselves.

A few tables away, Dolores spots Espe. It can't be her, of course. Dolores shakes her head and closes her eyes. When she opens her eyes, Espe is gone. After all these years, Dolores still feels her wife's spirit close by.

She digs into her burrito, and the refried beans spread in her mouth. The subtle blend of herbs and spices tickle her taste buds. She has to blink away tears.

"You can eat slowly, Dolores," Shig says. "Nobody will steal your food here."

Dolores nods, trying to swallow.

"Toma agua, mi'ja," the elderly woman in the white huipil says, handing her a water bottle across the table.

Dolores takes a sip to wash down the mouthful of beans. She recalls her abuela wore a similar huipil.

"The refried beans are vegetarian," the woman says with a smile. "They contain no pork fat."

"That's great," Dolores says.

Unlike the synthetic kind back home, every ingredient is grown in the camp. Doña Lupe would have loved it here. Even so, many American refugees still complain about the spicy food.

"What's your book about?" Shig asks.

Children his age never had the chance to visit bookstores or libraries. The tech conglomerates stopped producing physical books altogether in favor of digital counterparts, over forty states defunded their public libraries, and the Blackout wiped out what was left, all before they were born. She wonders if her book is the first Shig has ever held.

"It's called *Hang on to Hope*."

A large buzz circles above her head, and Dolores drops her fork, sudden visions blotting out reality. AI drones. The hum of death.

She shoves back from the table, metal grating against concrete. Singed flesh assaults her nostrils, plunges down her throat. She can't breathe.

"Watch out, Shig!" She ducks and gestures for him to do the same. When she closes her eyes, mangled corpses strewn across the road flood her mind. Screams pierce her ears. The drones always go for the heads first.

"Are you okay?"

Dolores opens her eyes, and the drones are gone. The dead bodies, the blood, gone. In its place, her fellow refugees eat, talk, and laugh. Birds chirp. A teenage girl beside her looks concerned, and Dolores can barely endure the pity in her eyes.

"It's just a honeybee. Try this." She hands Dolores an herb pouch. "When I get nervous, I smell it and calm down."

The scent reminds Dolores of Espe's skin, and she presses the bundle to her nose, counting ten breaths to collect herself.

"Thank you," she says, slowly recovering.

"You should see Dra. Flores."

"Excuse me?" Dolores frowns.

"She gave me the pouch. You can keep it if you like."

"Thank you."

"I'm Lucero," the girl says.

She reminds Dolores of another Lucero, her tenth-grade classmate with an incandescent smile. She remembers how deep dimples appeared in both cheeks when Lucero grinned.

"My abuela and I used to live in Horizon City," Lucero continues, pointing to the elderly woman in the huipil. "I used to have nightmares, too, but Dra. Flores has helped me a great deal."

Dolores doesn't answer, hands still shaking under the table, but Lucero keeps speaking, undaunted.

"As you know, gender-affirming care was banned in Texas. My abuela…" Lucero glances toward the elderly woman. "She tried to get me contraband estrogen pills, but —"

"They were rationed by AI," Dolores says.

"Right." Lucero pauses for a brief moment before continuing. "Dra. Flores is helping me with that, too."

"Glad to hear that."

"She went to medical school in Houston, but she's also a curandera. She uses herbs and natural products to treat her patients."

"Really?" Dolores leans forward with interest. "My abuela also had an herb garden."

"Dra. Flores is great," Lucero says, her voice bouncy and energetic. "Say hello for me if you see her."

"Okay," Dolores answers.

"It's strange to say this, but I'm happy here." Lucero flashes Dolores a bright smile before resuming her animated chat with her abuela.

Setting the bundle of herbs by her tray, Dolores picks up her fork. Shig is staring at her, and her cheeks grow warm. She feels unmoored. No one is a stranger to loss, but vulnerability is difficult for her in a way it never was for Espe. As if plucking the thought from her mind, Shig's smile is oddly assuring.

"Don't worry, Dolores," he says. "Everyone's really nice here, even when scary things happen. Even the bees are nice, I promise! They're harmless unless threatened. That's what Dra. Flores told us."

"The bees have returned," Dolores says, imagining a crowded hive. "That means the colony is healthy again." Hopefully, decreased human activity will continue reducing global warming. "That's good news." Maybe the Blackout was worth it; it was probably the only way to save Earth.

"Did you learn science at school?" Shig asks. "Did you like it?"

"Science wasn't my strong suit. I preferred humanities and social sciences. I was a librarian."

"Librarian?"

"I practically grew up in the library, so it was only natural that I became a librarian. I loved being surrounded by books." She spreads her arms to indicate shelves stretching in every direction.

Libraries across America became targets of violence, and a zealous mob burned down hers in broad daylight. Police were sent to protect the mob. Some nights, she still wakes from her nightmares of the fire.

"Before digital books replaced physical ones, of course," Dolores adds.

Shig takes another bite and washes it down with his drink. His eyes glow with curiosity.

"After the books were gone, did you lose your job?"

"No. Not exactly. After all the books were digitized, we sent our patrons into them."

"How?"

"Have you ever heard of metaverse books?"

"Like interactive movies?" Shig scrunches his nose. Dolores can see why he's confused. The internet had been dead for years by the time he became old enough to go to school.

"Something like that," Dolores says. "You could go inside a book and experience the story firsthand."

"Cool."

"Only as a tertiary character, so you couldn't interfere with the plot."

"Interesting," Shig says as if trying to sound polite.

"But I had to quit when I realized the bots were spewing propaganda and lies."

"I don't blame you," Shig says. "I'd do the same."

"Still, I missed the physical books," Dolores says with a sigh. "I hope the library system will come back someday."

"Maybe not the virtual system," Shig says, "but physical libraries. Virtual ones would be vulnerable to bot attacks."

"Right." Dolores nods. *You sound just like Espe, Shig.*

The incessant chatter around her drowns out the rest of her thoughts. Both fall silent and focus on the food.

"Let's go," Dolores says when they finish. They return their trays to the makeshift kitchen and step toward the garden. Wild potatoes have overtaken the flowerbeds. Cheers and laughter erupt from children playing some kind of chasing game. The kids have proved more resilient than the grown-ups.

"You haven't told me what your book is about," Shig says, squinting in the sunlight.

"I'll tell you what," Dolores says and takes out her book. "We can read it together, if you like."

"Will you teach me to read?" Shig says as she hands him the book.

"Sure," Dolores says. "We can start today."

Shig beams his brightest smile.

There's no school in the camp, but maybe Dolores can start one. A sudden breeze blows around her feet as if to tell her Espe's spirit is close by.

"I wonder if I can write a book someday."

"You can write about yourself. Someone will want to read it."

Shig nods.

"By the way, call me Lola." Adiós Dolores. She'll live with sorrow and pain for the rest of her life, but Lola is who she is.

"Okay, Lola."

Dolores gazes at the blue sky, warmth blooming in her chest at the realization that Shig will soon step into her world through reading.

"You were right, Espe," Dolores says as soon as Shig is out of earshot. "Surviving is our best revenge. I just hate that I have to start over without you." Her face clouds for a moment before she looks up.

As she watches Shig run toward the other children, she can't help but smile.

PUNKS4PALESTINE

Hereafter, Inc.

by Mohamed Shalabi

Washington D.C.

Adam's profile blew up across the smooth, white exterior of the Department of Security and Pre-violations building as Mara drew near. She could smell the electric current bouncing off the screen, like burnt plastic that made her nostril hairs stand. She paused in the heat, gradually lifting her gaze to the massive moving image of her son feeling shaken. The shadow of the Washington monument's tip, repurposed as the Eagle's Eye server tower, the heart of the city's surveillance, skewered his skull like a sword. Seconds later, the words *Enemy Subdued* flashed beneath Adam's face, like the shadows had spelled out his sentence. She gasped as a current shot through her heart, stopping it for a few seconds. Her eyes burned and she bit her lip until the burn subsided. She tasted blood.

They are lying, she thought and quickly buried that thought. Somehow, she could do that, forget tiny details of her life, simply by pressing a finger behind her ear where she could just about feel the Vagus nerve chip buried beneath her flesh.

It wasn't working as effectively now that she was faced with Adam's image and his sentence.

131

PUNKS4PALESTINE

Her eyes lingered upon his face, studying his droopy eyes, taut skin, straight hair, remembering how she used to tousle it with her fingers when he was young enough to sit in her lap, wishing it were curly like her own. She had recorded that memory, saved it in his profile and uploaded it to the EE. Back then, she assumed it would come in handy as a tool for reflection. Something that would help Adam on his path to immortality.

His face melted into the wall and reemerged with the guilt-ridden profiles of two other men and one woman. In her brain, she scrolled through the rolodex of names and faces of her son's acquaintances, but these faces didn't make an appearance.

He shouldn't be there.

Suddenly, a virtual flame burst through the screen, red and hot and real enough, she could feel its heat upon her skin, consuming the four profiles into virtual ash. A few of the passersby gasped before resuming their excursion. Behind her, the whole of the city including its mobile and airborne drones, was watching the wall and the face of her son being broadcast, shamed. They were watching her reaction too, to see if she would do anything drastic. No one acted drastically since Hereafter Inc. the company she started and sold to the DOSP, became part of their lives. Back then, twenty years ago, she was named a pioneer of a new industry that revitalized security in America by introducing a credit system that made people reconsider the choices they made in life...or suffer a lifetime, and afterlife, of pain.

Welcome to Hereafter Inc. Where you can literally go to hell if you step out of line.

As Mara had expected, a camera lens winked at her just a few inches away, and she strained, fumbled to turn her frown into a smile until her face hurt. She reluctantly glanced at her wrist where a subcutaneous number, a result of the credit-chip planted there since her company started operating, flashed in green.

I am still safe, she thought and allowed herself an exhale.

Inside the building, cool air blasted across her face, but it wasn't enough to quench the burning heat inside her. The scuffle of feet against the tiles and the small chatter she was used to hearing from her former workplace, former as of last week, was deafening now and somewhat of a nuisance. She watched all the feigned smiles on the faces around her and her stomach turned like she'd eaten something rotten. She continued past the crowds, past the courier bots towards her office, wondering if it too had changed in a week's time. She hoped not. As a contractor for the DOSP, she acknowledged the underlying issues of bureaucracy, namely that of time and was optimistic about her office, her belongings still being where they were since she'd 'resigned'.

PUNKS4PALESTINE

Down the main corridor where only a few people and bots trailed by, the colorful posters of Hereafter Inc. that lined the dull walls flashed with messages she authored or otherwise signed off on.

She focused on the fire-orange posters that oozed with ominous tones, featuring men and women escaping an inferno blazing behind them in a pit.

Protect your State. Protect your fate. Hereafter Inc.

The sky-blue posters were calmer, featuring men and women wearing toothy grins, too wide to be normal, overlooking an endless forest enclosing a crisp lake, and bordered by tall glass buildings that touched the sky.

You'll Be in Safe Hands for Eternity. Upgrade Today If You Qualify. Hereafter Inc.

Adam should have been there, she thought, and continued on into the bowels of the building where she was bombarded with more preachy posters that made her feel deep disdain for her past self.

Watch yourself like someone else is watching. One read, depicting a man stashing a gun in his pocket with obvious shame while the eyes of the Washington Monument, the EE, squinted at him.

Her skin prickled the closer she drew to her office. She wished she were elsewhere.

A new guard, tall and built like a wall, was standing by the automated turnstiles when she appeared in the narrow hall that cut through the building. The bars, yellow and labeled with *Authorized Personnel Only* warnings, were shut. She adjusted her wrist until the subcutaneous chip's outline was green, visible. The guard squinted his no nonsense eyes at her.

When she swiped her wrist along the sensor it flashed red. His eyes met hers.

Perhaps she was wrong about bureaucracy after all.

"I don't know why it's not working, but I have an appointment with Rita Wells," Mara explained before he could ask, and with nimble fingers, she rubbed the nub where the chip was burrowed. And what the hell did she expect? That they would welcome her back with open arms after what Adam had almost done? Her skin turned hot and a sheen of sweat broke across her forehead.

"Is she expecting you, ma'am?" the man said, his voice steady, but bordering on suspicion. He turned to face her, crossing his arms, as if to prepare himself to eject her should need be. Did he know about Adam too, or was he just a hired henchman?

A second camera lens winked from his badge. They were everywhere, studying everyone's expressions and thoughts. Judging.

The score on her wrist was still green.

"Yes. Can you please let her know I'm here?" she said and flashed him a smile.

He nodded as if speaking was too taxing. As if she were inconveniencing him. But he could not refuse to do his job. His wrist flashed green as well. He clicked a button on his shoulder and asked the necessary questions. Within a few seconds, the guard swiped his wrist along the sensor and the gate opened.

"Thank you so much!" She barely held her smile. Then she adjusted her purse beneath her armpit and scrambled off, hoping she didn't look too guilty. The purse felt heavier than usual. She hoped the bag of sugar inside didn't spill.

Sunlight poured into the corridor where her office was located away from public access. On weekdays, the doors were open to all employees, but Mara had to make the appointment soon and preferably when she and Rita could speak alone. She couldn't shake the feeling of being a stranger in her old building even when the electronic placard outside her office still projected her name.

Mara Faruq. Creative Projects Director. Hereafter Inc.

When they approached her about her resignation, they did it in person. Such matters were usually left for bots or holo-mail. But her time as a contractor, as long as it was, was valuable to the DOSP despite the danger Adam represented. The process had to be more personal.

She could still remember how hot her face had turned upon hearing the news. All at once. That she was fired and that her son was accused of a pre-violation crime.

She opened the door and poked her head through. The lingering scent of jasmine and white lily reminded her of staying late nights to perfect her project. The present she crafted for Adam when he turned 20. His own virtual heaven. It was in her office where it'd always been. Almost complete, but good enough to host him.

Looking over her shoulder and finding no one around, she slipped in. There were no cameras this deep into the building. It made the employees of the DOSP uncomfortable. Plus, Mara always amused herself with the ironic thought of being under the gaze of the eye that she and her team had built. Lucky for her, the department had trusted its workers to do their jobs without being burdened by micromanaging.

Adam's scent lingered at the threshold. Deodorant and sweat combating for dominance.

When he was still a child, he used to crawl into her office just to scare her and she pretended to be alarmed. She could almost see his shadow there, his prints in the carpet. Her eyes burned.

The walls, egg-white, were barely visible beneath the schematics of virtual worlds she'd crafted. Their names were handwritten in a corner at the top. Words only she could understand.

Paradise Lost, Jannah, the land of milk and honey, and more and more. There were others too, borne of her imagination and the stories her father used to tell her back when she was a little girl. Paradises and infernos in holy books that either enticed or deterred people into performing certain actions. The same principles she instilled in her concepts. In the past, those worlds were uncertain, unreal, but she brought them to life through long hours of work and complex strings of algorithms. There, in the corner of one of the schemes was scribbled Adam's name. She touched it, as if it would reach out to her and yanked it off the wall leaving a butterfly of paper stuck to the pin. With a straining heart, she folded the scheme and slipped it into her purse.

No one would notice it was gone. No one would care.

Before she could leave, she checked her drawers for her prized project. Adam's present, and found it stashed at the back of a binder, away from sight. She never told anyone about it. The virtual heaven normally sold for millions, was purchased by people who could afford the upgrade, people who had the money or the credits. But she was the owner of the company and she could craft whatever virtual heaven or hell she wanted.

Remembering it in her purse, she extracted the still sealed bag of sugar and refilled her personal sugar shaker, the one Rita adored, which resembled a small replica of an ancient Egyptian canopic jar that she left atop her desk. She took the jar with her and left the office for good.

Rita's office was across from her own. After two light knocks, the woman opened the door with a smile. She didn't have to put on a smile, but she did anyways.

Rita was younger than her by a few years, still in her late thirties, but work had transformed her face. Whoever said that the AI boom would lessen human suffering was a fool. Thin wisps of grey hairs defiantly poked from her bun, tinted her tar-black eyebrows.

"I was beginning to think you wouldn't come," she said, moving out of the way to let Mara in. Mara didn't smile.

"It wasn't easy, I have to admit. But I need to get some things off my chest," Mara said, walking toward her usual seat without invitation, feeling the weight in her chest multiply like a stone. She liked Rita's office because it always smelled like ground coffee. Before she was let go, they used to sit together at her desk and sip coffee while conversing about the old days, trading anecdotes, and stories of their children. Now, the office looked bleak. The live posters plastered all around the building decorated the walls, changing every few minutes. Once blue and green, once orange and red. Even the smell of coffee turned stale and rotten.

"No, I'm glad you came. Really. I mean, I'm sorry for everything you've been through recently," Rita said without looking at her.

She wasn't sorry, Mara thought. Her children were still alive and her job was secure. Rita was just being professional, so unlike herself. That was when Mara noticed the camera mounted atop her colleague's computer screen. It was watching her. Watching them both.

Mara fixed her smile again, ignoring the cramp that was starting at the edges of her lips.

"I was just as surprised as you were when the news came out." Rita placed her hand across her chest, as if she were the one having breathing problems.

Mara smirked. *Were you?* She wanted to say but locked the words behind her lips.

"But you know these tragedies just creep up on us when we least expect them to."

"I'm sorry. I don't want to take too much of your time, Rita," Mara said, with a hint of impatience. She wondered if the camera caught that much. "I just want us to get right to business, if you don't mind."

Rita looked taken aback for a second before her expression melted into a smile. "Of course, of course." She nodded and her fingers swiped across the large screen that sat above her desk. "Let me just pull up your file."

"You mean Adam's file." That hint of defiance in her voice released a bit of tension inside her.

"Yes, of course," Rita said and whispered. "Adam's file."

The space between them was suddenly filled with unspoken words and the heat Mara had radiated all day. Rita tapped her screen a few more times and in rolled a small electronic robot. It looked like a small fridge, encased in black glass. A red light flashed through its facade like an eye as it inched toward her. It could see her too, hear her. Another set of eyes and ears.

"That was quick." Rita said, reaching for the courier bot. She clicked a button on its smooth surface and a small mechanical drawer opened. From it, she pulled a long, black device that Mara recognized as a memory chip reader. She held back a gasp as her own memory flicked back to when she saw the device the first time after her father died. When the doctors planted his Vagus chip inside it.

Her father had commanded her not to do so, he wanted to die and get it over with, as he so jokingly phrased it. But dying, falling into the void where time and space cease to exist, was against the law. Since her company struck that deal with the government, uploading one's consciousness to the mainframe postmortem became mandatory.

"Why is he archived?" Mara asked, watching Rita unsheathe the black device. No one was ever meant to be saved in an archive.

Rita took the device that contained her son's Vagus nerve chip, essentially his entire being, and clicked it into her computer screen. There was a ding.

"The state classifies him as state property."

Mara's vision narrowed until it was like looking down a tube. She did not expect this impasse. Had she really thought she could obtain Adam that easily?

"State property?" Her voice was but a whisper.

Rita pretended like she was busy, fixing her eyes to the screen so that she wouldn't have to register Mara's contempt. "Criminals...people involved in a crime; especially major ones are required by law to remain within the confines of the state."

Something inside Mara popped, unleashing a fire that flared from her nose. She ignored the camera lens pointed at her face. She didn't care, in fact, that it was pointed at her face. She didn't even realize that she was on her feet again, closing the space between her and Rita with her craning neck and her hot breath.

"You know damn well Adam isn't a criminal. He didn't commit any crimes."

Shocked and speechless, Rita's eyes flitted to the camera. A nervous smile broke across her lips.

"That verdict was decided by the EE, unfortunately. I had nothing to do with it. You know this."

"EE is just a machine, Rita. It can make mistakes. Hereafter is my invention. It's not perfect."

"That's not highly likely. The algorithm is perfectly efficient. And ever since its inception, crime has gone down exponentially. Almost 100 percent." Rita composed her tone every time it rose or fell, trying to maintain a professional attitude. Her eyes continued to dart back and forth between the camera and Mara's moist eyes, like she was warning her.

Sit down, control your temper, or you'll be dragged out of here.

Mara did just that. She assumed her composure, biting down on the truths she wanted to hurl all at once, in no coherent fashion. Her temples throbbed with the pressure of them wanting out.

"Let me remind you that EE is an infallible system. Everything that was put into its programming came from years of legal canon that was fool-proofed over the course of humanity." Rita continued, sitting back in her seat, and knotting her hands together. "It's your baby. Are you telling me you deliberately sabotaged your invention? I won't believe it."

Mara stared at her, then at her knuckles which had turned white and pink, like her skin would split and bleed. Her wrist flashed green still. She thought of another plan. A plan to infiltrate the mainframe and rescue Adam from his infernal fate. She stared back at the device which was attached to the computer screen, contemplating how her son's identity and memories were nothing more than shots of electric current passing between semiconductors and nanochips.

An argument formed in her mind. At least there, no one could hear her thoughts. That wasn't entirely correct. The cameras were fitted with magnetic brain scanners and emotion sensors.

The single camera glared at her, uploading every muscle twitch into the EE, translating those expressions into sins and deeds, and uploading them to the Hereafter app. The system was meant to uphold law in a world of fallible lawlessness, yet it was anything but fool proof. Even Adam with his minimal hacking experience could break into the mainframe and switch things around without the AI detecting it. She glared right back at the camera, wanting to dive through it and rip EE's wires from the mainframe. She wanted to destroy Hereafter Inc like it destroyed her son. Or did Adam bring this on himself with his inquiries and anti-surveillance rhetoric?

"You know who he is, Rita. You know he's a good boy." Mara was convinced of this, but Rita looked uncertain.

She opened her mouth only to close it again, then turned her attention to the screen.

"He wouldn't ever harm anyone. I know him well enough."

Rita turned the monitor around so that Mara could take a glimpse of what she was researching.

There, she spotted an illuminated scan of a brain. Adam's name was labeled in the top right corner. This was her son. Reduced now to a trillion, trillion pinpricks of light and neuronal causeways stored onto a thumb-sized drive.

"We can review the footage together, if you like."

Mara inched closer to the screen. She fixated on a few neuronal connections that stood out brighter than the rest in the occipital and prefrontal cortex, labeled with a series of acronyms. PFLTP2, MTLTP45, PLTP50, HLTP24. Someone had highlighted those areas on purpose. Rita touched one of the points in the prefrontal cortex. The brain map vanished behind a word document.

"This was recovered most recently before the sentence."

Mara squinted her eyes at the gobble of words, trying to make sense of them.

"It's a procedures list. The EE chip records sequences from the prefrontal cortex into code, into words. So, if you look here..." Rita ran her finger along a string of words.

Meet with Marcus to get guns and ammo.

Mara couldn't believe what she was reading. She didn't want to believe it. These couldn't be her son's words, thoughts. He would never--

"He was planning something, Mara. Marcus was the other suspect and when he was arrested, he was in possession of a large cache of weapons and ammo in his home."

"But he couldn't have. I was with him all along."

"Which brings me to my next point." Rita closed the message screen and clicked a point in the occipital lobe, labeled OLTP141. "Watch this."

The screen changed to a video player and Mara blinked nonchalantly, praying in her mind that it was nothing incriminating.

The screen was focused on an alley, somewhere in DC. She recognized the buildings that were pressed together like multicolored bricks and the garbage containers filled to the brim, about to spill over. The footage moved toward a dark niche wedged between the two buildings, barely visible. There, three people, two men and a woman she recognized from the poster outside, were sipping on cigars and blowing smoke circles. They smiled as the person behind the lens approached and the man, Marcus, lifted his shirt to reveal a gun.

"We're ready when you are, fresh meat."

Then Adam's voice spoke loud and clear, like they were inside his head.

"I'm ready. Meet me around 8:30 near the EE monument. Mom's work is close by. I have access to the building. We can start there."

But the footage stopped short before Adam could say anything else.

"That's not my son," Mara said, shaking her head. She couldn't believe her own words. The voice in the video

146

was Adam's, but without seeing his face, she couldn't be certain. "It's a fake."

The dam that held back Mara's torrent of tears broke. Camera or not, she couldn't care less. She wanted the eye to know that she was angry over her son's loss and the injustice he was delivered.

"It's a fake. Adam would never do that. Never."

But as those words spilled out, she drew back into a memory of her own from last year. When Adam came into her office and candidly informed her of his dissatisfaction with the kingdom she had ruled over.

"Grandpa told me people used to be free back then. They could say or do whatever they wanted without being punished for it."

Mara had warned him never to speak those words again.

But he stormed out of her office that day without promising anything.

Rita raised both her hands in the air. "Please, Mara. You're making a scene."

Mara knocked the camera off her desk. "I don't care, Rita. Goddamn it. You know my son, for crying out loud. You took care of him. You know he's a good boy."

Rita fumbled to stand the camera again. "Calm down, Mara. Lemme get you a cup of coffee. Please let's talk about this calmly."

Mara slumped back into her seat, sobbing, and hugging her purse. She couldn't spend another minute in that office.

"Please," she whispered. Her voice tinny and strained, like she was choking. "I can vouch for him. Take my credits. It should be enough."

Rita looked like she wanted to cry too. Her expressions softened and so did her tone when she said, "I don't think that's possible, Mara. He's been convicted."

A moment later, the same robot entered the room, this time with two cups of coffee in its belly.

Rita passed one over to Mara, like she used to in the old days. Mara clutched her purse, dug her hand into it and extracted the canopic jar.

Rita glanced at her determinately. "Drink. You'll feel a lot better." She moved to sit beside her now. "I know how hard this is, I swear and I wish there was something I could do."

Was she still pretending for the camera, or was she being genuine. It was hard to tell.

Mara wiped her tears with her sleeve and opened the jar. Rita instinctively took two spoonful's like she always did and sprayed them into her cup. Mara took none.

"You're right," Mara said, sniffling and nodding at the same time, imagining the virtual inferno she programmed and Adam being tossed into it. A pit of black fire. Scorpions and snakes as large as hills. Endless torment and pain. "There's clear evidence. I can't refute that. I just wished I could've done something about it earlier."

Rita didn't say anything but stirred her coffee with the tablespoon. She couldn't deny her friend's words knowing they were true. Instead, she took a sip of her drink and looked pensively toward the door, like she was thinking of a solution. She had her free hand on Mara's shoulder and she caressed it coldly, just for show. Mara watched the green light shine on her wrist and hated how it made her pretend.

"He was never happy with the system," Mara said. She remembered the days she'd spent crafting his heaven in her office, staying up late to add the details, every single leaf and blade of grass, every single river and cloud. All for Adam. It was his own abode for when he died an old man. A costly gift that could've well belonged to a billionaire. "He wanted to be just like his grandfather. He couldn't believe a world like the old world existed."

Rita nodded, saying, "yeah" and "I understand" a lot and sipped her coffee.

"Mothers just want their children to be happy, you know," Mara said. Rita yawned. "I would've done anything for my son."

Within seconds, Rita's eyes rolled back into her head and she fell back onto the floor with a thud. Mara quickly got to her feet, knocked the camera off its tripod and bent over Rita to make sure she was breathing.

"I'm sorry," she whispered before dashing to her computer. The computer was still logged into the mainframe and that was all that mattered now.

She typed commands across the screen, slashed her index right and left, scouring through the files to find Adam, while glancing sideways at the camera.

Her wrist flashed from green to red.

Her heart stopped beating and all breathable air left the room.

What did I expect?

Blood rushed inside her head like waves crashing along a rocky shore. The pressure in her temples was almost too much to handle and her head spun. Her father's voice, muffled by the cacophony that took over the serenity inside the room, reminded her that it was better to be dead than unfree.

He had told her about his world and how it had died the day people gave up their freedom for false security. She didn't listen to him, choosing instead to go along with her crusade...to build a safer future for her children and the children of the nation.

Her father was right.

Adam knew this too.

How was she so stupid to assume that Adam's safety was paramount to all. That it was above his freedom and happiness. He was never happy until he could think freely, without boundaries. And she had always tried to silence him. For his safety.

Scouring the files paid off as soon as she found the right one.

I'm coming for you, she thought to herself, blood rushing in her ears. *I'm gonna save you.*

She prayed that no one would be alerted to her transgression. Prayed the giant guard at the gate would stay put until she was done transferring Adam's consciousness into the virtual home she built for him.

The file opened.

She paused. Gasped. Fell into her seat when she spotted Adam, the virtual avatar that housed his consciousness, being flayed in his virtual hell by surgical machines. Unanesthetized, he screamed as his skin was slowly peeled away from his muscle and bone. She shut the file, her own sobs ricocheting off the walls. Her hands trembled, jerking her fingers across the screen. Her chest caved in on itself leaving her with no air to breathe.

Adam didn't deserve what they were doing to him. The accusation was a hoax, she was sure of it. She'd heard rumors about hackers corrupting, hijacking, and tinkering with memories...for political reasons. How was this situation any different?

She yanked the memory device from its slot, removed her son's Vagus nerve chip from within it, a drop of his blood had clotted around its edges, and planted it into her own memory device where heaven was crafted. The Hereafter Inc. logo carved onto the device, a remnant of her old days, shimmered.

Then she plugged it back into the screen.

Opening the file, Adam's avatar traipsed into the heaven she'd created for him. Smile on his face, pain gone. He looked back, into the screen, as if looking at his mother, and smiled.

She caressed his face through the glass. Brushed back his thick brown eyebrows. Studied his dimples carefully and tried to tousle his hair into curls.

A laugh rose inside her as her chest filled with a cool breeze that consumed her slowly, slowly. But soon, a knock shook the door.

"Ma'am, are you alright in there?"

Mara chose not to speak but swiped away at the computer screen and uploaded the file to the mainframe. If she could plant it there, then it would be safe for eternity. If she could plant it there, then she would also unleash the virus that would destroy every other heaven and hell in existence.

And the world would be free again.

Author Bios

May Haddad is an Arab American writer of speculative fiction whose work deals with the Arab experience across time and space and touches on themes of nostalgia, isolation, memory, and longing. As of this publication, you can find her work in The Markaz Review and Nightmare Magazine.

R.J. Breathnach is a Wexford-born writer based in Meath, Ireland. His fiction has been published in *Sparks Literary Journal*, *Andromeda Literary Magazine*, and *The Honest Ulsterman*, among others. His debut poetry chapbook, *I Grew Tired of Being a Zombie*, was published by Alien Buddha Press in 2021. In his free time he enjoys reading science-fiction novels and losing to a computer at chess.

Emma Burnett is a researcher and writer. She has had stories in Nature:Futures, Mythaxis, Northern Gravy, Apex, Radon, Utopia, MetaStellar, Milk Candy Review, Roi Fainéant, JAKE, and more. You can find her @slashnburnett, @slashnburnett.bsky.social, or emmaburnett.uk.

Christopher R. Muscato is a writer from Colorado, winner of the XR Wordsmith Solarpunk Storytelling Showcase, and Terra.do climate fellow. His recent stories can be found in Shoreline of Infinity, House of Zolo, and Solarpunk Magazine.

In addition to their work at Solarpunk Magazine, as a poetry editor, and at Android Press, as an editor, **J.D. Harlock**'s writing has been featured in Strange Horizons, New York University's Library of Arabic Literature, and the SFWA Blog. You can find them on Twitter, Threads, & Instagram @JD_Harlock.

Abigail Guerrero is an aroace, ND and ESL/EFL author from Mexico. Her work has appeared or is forthcoming in Bloodless: An Anthology of Blood-free horror, The Voidspace, Exposed Bone, Simultaneous Times and Radon Journal. You can find her on Twitter as: @_gail_guerrero.

R.L. Summerling (she/her) is a part-time fiction writer and full-time squirrel watcher from Southeast London. An author of dark, decadent speculative fiction, her work is full of unease, anxiety and excess.

Eric Farrell is a beer vendor by day, and speculative fiction author by night. His writing credits stem from a career in journalism, where he reported for a host of college, local, and metro newspapers in the Los Angeles area. Find more of his work in with Aphotic Realm, Stupefying Stories, and Haven Spec.

Toshiya Kamei (they/them) is an Asian writer who takes inspiration from fairy tales, folklore, and mythology. Their short fiction has appeared in *Daily Science Fiction, Galaxy's Edge, and elsewhere. Their piece "Hungry Moon" won Apex Magazine's October 2022 Microfiction Contest.*

Mohamed (Moe) Shalabi is a Palestinian-American author of literary and speculative fiction, neuroscientist, and former junior literary agent. Moe's stories are inspired by his diverse background and upbringing in the Middle East. His writing appears in multiple literary magazines such as the Nonbinary Review, Reed, and Superstition Review. His short story Palestina was nominated for a Pushcart Prize. When he's not working on his multiple manuscripts, Moe works as a full-time consultant in Washington, D.C. Moe is represented by Kat Kerr of the Donald Maass Literary Agency. You can follow him on twitter/X @Agent_Moe or learn more about him on his website www.MoeShalabi.com.

Marc Ruvolo (he/him) is a queer writer and musician living in Portland, Oregon who once considered himself a punk. He founded the seminal Bucket O' Blood book store in Chicago, and his poetry and fiction have appeared in *Cynthia Pelayo's Gothic Blue Book Series, The Night's End Horror Podcast,* and *The Best of Abyss & Apex Vol. 4*, to name a few. His debut horror novella, "SLOE," was released in 2023 by Unnerving Books. A second queer horror novella, "Pieties," is available now from Off Limits Press. Find him on twitter at @RuvFur.

PUNKS4PALESTINE

Logan O'Connor is a gay/queer punk who has been publishing fanzines, writting articles, stories, prose, and artwork that focuses on their love of punk rock, diy, and horror. His art has been featured in many punk and art magazines. He is also currently putting together a cultural magazine called Final Guy in March '24. You can check out some of his artwork on instagram @loganoconnorgallery

Jasen Bacon is an Appalachian word nerd. Founder and editor at Hyphenpunk, he is also slightly obsessed with space ships and laser guns.